A STRANGE NOTE TO FINISH ON

A STRANGE NOTE TO FINISH ON

FRICKER'S FIRST CASE

ALAN NORMAN

Matador
9 Priory Business Park
Kibworth Beauchamp
Leicestershire LE8 0RX, UK
Tel: (+44) 116 279 2299
Fax: (+44) 116 279 2277
Email: books@troubador.co.uk
Web: www.troubador.co.uk/matador

ISBN 978 1783061 013

British Library Cataloguing in Publication Data.
A catalogue record for this book is available from the British Library.

This is a work of fiction. All characters, locations and events are imaginary, and any
resemblance to actual persons, locations and events is purely coincidental.

Typeset in 11pt Aldine401 BT Roman by Troubador Publishing Ltd, Leicester, UK
Printed and bound in the UK by TJ International, Padstow, Cornwall

Matador is an imprint of Troubador Publishing Ltd

MIX
Paper from
responsible sources
FSC   FSC® C013056
www.fsc.org

For Angie

CHAPTER 1

Stella Maitland lent back in the old wooden rocking chair and gazed out through the rain-stained patio doors on to the rear garden. Gently stroking her fingers through the thick black hair of her beard she quietly contemplated her eight decades of life. Her wrinkled features grimaced as she recalled the lovers, then with a sigh Stella mentally corrected herself, remembering that, although she had indulged in a second short relationship with Percy Thatcher before he was tragically and fatally torpedoed close to the Balearics in 1942, he still could only be classed as a singular and quite forgettable lover. She paused in her thoughts then smiled faintly as her fuddled mind summoned up a faded image of her faithful poodle Rex, a true, but now long-dormant friend who could always be relied on in times of trouble.

Stella hadn't worn particularly well; two new hips and constant back pain troubled her daily, but at eighty-two and to be still spouting a full chin of hair was in her mind a fine achievement.

She had lived in Scotswood Manor, a residential home predominately for ladies of the arts, for seventeen years and still did not tire of the bohemian ambiance that pervaded the dark grey granite walls of the Victorian pile. Its changeable atmosphere reflected both the weather and her moods. Moods that ranged from the dull and miserable to bright and sunny on an almost daily basis.

In her early years Stella had been a promising trombonist; however, an unfortunate accident with a vigorously closing door, the

1

instrument and her front teeth had put an end to her ambitions. There followed forty plus years of musical torture, as first a teacher then head of arts at a succession of secondary schools, until retirement and Scotswood saved what was left of her sanity.

It was these troubled memories and her present obsession with the brown circles on the lawn left by Otto, the Doberman belonging to the home's domestic, Mrs Langton, that occupied Stella's mind as she gently rocked to and fro, oblivious to everything else around her.

She was so oblivious that she didn't hear the door handle turn. She didn't see the dark gloved hand pick up the small bronze bust of Mozart, or hear the soft footsteps approach across the room until a familiar reflection in the door to the garden made her turn in surprise.

"That was a top C, definitely a top C," stated Hilda as she reflected thoughtfully on the ear-splitting sound that had woken her from her early afternoon slumber.

"No, you are quite wrong, more a B flat, my dear," commented Edna, her companion of almost thirty years and a lady to whom being right was a way of life.

"I wish whoever it was would do it again. I feel they failed to hold the note long enough for me to get a true idea of the sound," retorted Hilda; but even this early on in the conversation, Edna had lost interest and with a final "You never did have a good ear, top C my foot," she returned to her book.

Hilda and Edna occupied a spacious apartment on the second floor of Scotswood Manor's west wing, overlooking the same patch of garden that had absorbed so much of Stella Maitland's time. Both ladies were spinsters, by name and very much by nature. They detested men, who they believed vehemently, were horrible, dirty vermin with only one thing on their minds, although neither Edna nor Hilda had ever been told or even thought to find out quite what this one thing was.

The curmudgeonly couple spent most of their waking hours either arguing over nothing of consequence, then agreeing that Edna's opinion must be correct, or spying on the other residents of Scotswood.

The slightly splayed wheels of Martha Nixdorf's sturdy, chrome Zimmer frame moved slowly over the thick pile carpet of the Manor's ground floor hallway. Martha, an amply proportioned wide load, had not quite mastered control of her mobility aid. The deep ruts left in the beige carpet from her many previous journeys to visit her old friend Stella often caused her to lurch violently to the side. Both the paintwork and skirting boards showed numerous signs of past collisions and Martha smiled as she remembered the time she squashed Clive, Scotswood's handyman, between the walking frame, herself and the corner cabinet outside flat twenty-four. It had taken four firemen, a hoist and two and a half hours to free him and she felt certain that he hadn't been the same man since. In fairness, however, she reflected, he had always walked with a slight limp, but never supported by the stick that he now used constantly.

Martha usually took a full twenty minutes to cover the fifty-five yards between her door and Stella's flat. Today was different, however; having heard the strange, shrill sound that had appeared to come from the vicinity of her friend's rooms, she felt that, although not unduly alarmed, a little more haste was in order.

Martha rolled to a halt outside the white Georgian door of Stella's apartment in record time and knocked purposely. The door creaked; it was unlocked and slightly ajar. Puzzled by her security-conscious friend's apparent carelessness, she gave it a vigorous push and manoeuvred herself slowly into the small, dimly lit entrance hall.

Cautiously trundling forward, Martha called out in her broad coalfield accent, "Stella! Are you there, luv?"

An eerie silence pervaded the interior of the flat and, with no reply forthcoming, she began to feel more than a little concerned.

To her left were the doors to Stella's bathroom and bedroom. Martha moved past these and into the now brightly sunlit lounge where, over the years, the two of them had shared many happy hours reminiscing about the good old days.

"There it goes again, Edna! A top C if ever I heard one," exclaimed Hilda, erupting an avalanche of scone crumbs in the general direction of her exasperated companion.

"For the last time, my dear," snapped Edna, her hawklike eyes rising slowly above the rims of her thin gold spectacles. "That was not a top C. I suggest you have your ears reamed out, dear, before you drive me quite mad!"

"What did you say, Edna?" replied Hilda, but her question elicited no response as her friend was already immersed back in her book.

Martha Nixdorf swayed slowly, unsteadily lifting the wheels of her walking frame off the floor with each backward movement. The echo of her anguished cry still pounded in her mind as she tried hard to take in the horrible sight that had greeted her as she entered the lounge. Martha had always known that she wasn't the sharpest knife in the drawer, but even her simple mind knew that Stella was dead. Her friend's inert body lay, her face turned to one side, on the multicoloured floral carpet to the left of the now stationary rocking chair. A large, blood-soaked wound was visible just above the left ear.

It wasn't, however, the sight of blood that caused Martha to howl in fright; she had seen plenty of that before, growing up as she had over her father's slaughterhouse. No, it was the pained expression of confused terror on her friend's face and the lifeless staring eyes that left her shocked and unnerved.

Margaret Bronwyn-Jones, the resident cook, was first to run into flat thirty-two, closely followed by Langton and Donald S Ball,

Scotswood's ethereal proprietor. Clive, the handyman, shuffled along a good twenty yards behind.

"I heard the cry," lilted Margaret in an unusually deep voice that came straight from the valleys. "I came running see and, oh ye gods and little fishes!"

She stopped abruptly as her mind tried to absorb the awful scene before her.

Martha, oblivious to the commotion around her, swayed back and forth like a large bulbous pendulum while Stella, resembling a waxwork, stared, unmoving, unseeing.

"Someone call an ambulance," stammered Ball.

While all about looked at one another Langton calmly picked up the phone from the small side table and dialled 999.

Chapter 2

The small, cramped, dimly lit second floor office that Detective Inspector Giles Fricker reluctantly called his, overlooked Hampton le Heath's high street. The police station was cold, old and in decay and Fricker wanted out. He sincerely believed that he was born to better things; the Met, Scotland Yard, Chief of Police, the main man. He had no intention of wasting his Bramshill accelerated promotion and 2:2 degree on a backwater like Hampton le Heath. At thirty-eight years of age he felt that it was about time his potential was appreciated.

The need to succeed had been hammered into him at an early age. His father, a rather distant church-going pillar of society, had lavished his praise on Fricker's elder brother Brian. Brian was an exceptional academic who had gone from university to achieve great things in chemical research. Giles's all-consuming interest in tortoises paled into insignificance in comparison. He had meandered slowly, in the style of his pet (unimaginatively christened Terrance), through school and a zoology course at Bristol.

Those years, which, in the eyes of his elders, were seen as a time of underachievement, had an unfortunate effect on his personality. He became insular and was perceived by his few friends and acquaintances as arrogant; however, inside, unseen to the world there lurked an insatiable desire to do well and be loved.

"Who needs brains when you have an ego like yours" had been his university tutor's final words to him on graduation day. Fricker's confused mind had treasured this supposed compliment ever since.

6

With no obvious route into the world of testudines and the premature death in hibernation of Terrance, Fricker's life reached a sad crisis point.

He drifted without direction and there followed a period of casual, short-lived jobs: hearse driver, Father Christmas's elf and bingo caller; before, more through luck than judgement, a career in the police force began.

Stumbling by accident into the local Methodist hall one bleak Tuesday morning, Fricker inadvertently found himself at an under-subscribed police recruitment day. A short interview later and he was immersed in the selection process.

Surprisingly Fricker seemed to flourish in the regimented world of the force. After ten years and a relatively speedy ascent through the ranks, via postings that removed him "from the hair of his superiors" rather than recognised his abilities, Fricker had been singled out to take control of Hampton's small local CID unit. He struggled to comprehend why he had ended up in this backwater. All he could think was that it must be but a short interlude on his way to the top.

The shrill ring of the telephone in the office next door and the gruff, uncompromising tones of Detective Sergeant Tony O'Brien jolted Fricker from his daydream. *A bit of a rough diamond,* thought Fricker as he mused on the merits of his number two, *but not too bad at his job.* Then a word from the overheard conversation made him sit up and take notice.

A murder! Fricker was certain that was what O'Brien had said, a murder in Hampton le Heath, "Thank god for that," he exclaimed in delight. At last! A chance to show off his superior investigational skills.

"Scotswood Manor, sir," said O'Brien as he stood in the doorway of DI Fricker's office. "An elderly resident appears to have been beaten to death."

Fricker gasped inwardly; he had never had to deal with a crime as substantial as murder. Other serious incidents, yes, he mused, the theft of a child's bike and the Trinity Square flasher. Although much to his embarrassment the latter had turned out to be an unfortunate case of mistaken identity. Fricker's mind drifted off, as it was prone to do. He physically squirmed as he recalled the incident. How was he to know that a sharp gust of wind would have that effect on the vicar's robes?

"Are you alright, sir?" enquired O'Brien as Fricker stumbled back into the real world.

"Er, yes, O'Brien, Scotswood Manor you say... we'd best get over there."

O'Brien drove the four, leafy-laned miles to Scotswood at speed. Fricker gripped hard on the edge of his seat, his white bony knuckles almost protruding through his skin as he listened to his sergeant's report of the initial telephone call.

Much to Fricker's relief the pale grey saloon slid to an abrupt halt on the multi-flecked gravel outside the Manor's main entrance. O'Brien, a stocky six-foot ex-Army PT instructor strode purposely around from his side of the car and pressed the ornate, though tarnished, brass doorbell. A crescendo of chimes erupted from somewhere deep within the building. Fricker, meanwhile, was still extracting himself from the vehicle. He was a less-imposing figure than O'Brien, five foot nothing with the Fricker side of the family looks – unmanageable and unfashionable hair over a deep forehead, topping a long nose and protruding bottom lip that gave him a perpetual expression of unhappiness.

Having finally stumbled out of the car he was greeted at the now open door by a tall pale figure with the bearing of an underfed clergyman.

"Good afternoon, vicar," he began. "Fricker, Detective Inspector Fricker, and you are, sir?"

Ball, looking visibly shaken, spluttered out his answer. "D… Donald S Ball, proprietor of Scotswood… we've had a most awful event… a murder, Inspector… a dreadful murder!"

Fricker did not respond. He stood, absent-mindedly adjusting his attire while his mind, still mentally continuing to recover from the journey, wandered off. Sensing the lull in proceedings, O'Brien interjected in his usual tactful manner.

"Where's the body, Mr Ball?"

Having followed Ball through reception and down a long corridor, O'Brien and Fricker stood in the doorway and assessed the scene before them. Flat thirty-two was crowded. A wailing Welsh woman sat slumped in a rocking chair. A small group, consisting of Clive the limping handyman, Langton and the large swaying figure of Martha Nixdorf, watched intently as two paramedics attempted to pump life into the unresponsive body on the floor.

O'Brien, as normal, took the initiative. "Everybody out! Now! This is a murder scene, leave the professionals to their job," he bellowed.

Within seconds, after some initial huffing and puffing, the room cleared.

Pleased with the effectiveness of his request, O'Brien turned to speak to his boss, only to find that he also had vacated the room as instructed.

Having caught sight of the steadily retreating figure of his superior, O'Brien roared after him.

"Sir!"

Fricker, trying hard to find a way past the considerable bulk that was Martha Nixdorf, stopped in his tracks. He turned quickly and caught Ball a firm blow in the solar plexus with his bony elbow. Ball stumbled backwards, lost his balance and took the limping Clive, his stick and a still wailing Bronwyn-Jones through the open doorway of the linen cupboard. The wailing became a muffled drone as they were all engulfed in a plume of feathers.

Meanwhile Fricker, unaware of the chaos he had caused, returned to the side of his sergeant.

Having given up the fruitless task of resuscitation the two paramedics left, leaving O'Brien bent over the prone figure of Stella Maitland. He was pausing to view the now clotting wound, when a hand tapped him on the shoulder.

"Dr Body! About time, I thought you were stuck in the bar."

"No, Tony, busy with another incident, dead dog on Walpole Street, hit and run, nasty business. Made a right mess of the car, three series BMW, in a very nice shade of cream. Very sad, so what have we here?"

"Looks like a blow to the head," interjected Fricker with his usual astuteness.

"I can see you are firing on all cylinders, Giles," replied the police doctor.

A stout man in his early sixties with receding hair, Dr Ivor Boddicote, known to all as Dr Body, had been Hampton le Heath's police surgeon for over thirty years. During that time he had acquired a reputation for popping more pills than he prescribed. Occasionally though he had been known to stir his grey cells in to action, bringing to an investigation the odd word of wisdom. However, with the sun setting in his bespectacled blue eyes, these events were now, few and far between.

"The body, Body!" queried Fricker. "What do you think?"

"Oh, ah, yes, the body, dead, yes," he said sombrely. "I can categorically state she is dead."

After a pause for effect Dr Body continued, "And yes, Inspector Fricker, I believe the blow to the head did it."

Donald S Ball sat behind his sturdy mahogany desk, peered out through the wide bay window and tried hard to make sense of the day's events. The late afternoon rain had ceased and the early spring sunshine had returned, casting sprightly dancing shadows over the lawn and garden. *Such a beautiful day and yet all this sadness*, he thought to himself. His musings, however, did not last long. They were brought to an abrupt halt by a sharp knock at the door to his office, followed by the emergence into the room of the small, skinny figure that was Hillary Smallman; his assistant and long-term fiancée.

Ball, slightly startled, looked up and forced a strained smile.

"Hillary darling, what a mess!"

She stopped in her tracks, taking a sideways glance at her reflection in the tall wall mirror to her left. She knew that the mirror was cheap, from the local pound shop to be precise, and that it didn't give a true image. But to say she was a mess was a bit strong.

"Donald darling, I did my hair this morning, I thought…?"

"Not you, sweetkins," he replied. "The murder, the police, everything!"

Smallman looked relieved. She had never been a confident woman when it came to her looks; at four foot eleven, with a figure in which curves played no part, her plain features, broken up only by her hooked nose and horn-rimmed glasses, she was not what you would call a classical beauty.

She had been teased endlessly at school, home and in her previous employment as an assistant museum curator; a role where sadly, her desire to specialise in the Egyptians had ended in tragedy.

She grimaced as she remembered the night the security guard had unintentionally become locked in the temperature-controlled artefact store. Having been there for just under twelve hours he had eventually managed to make contact with the first person to arrive the following morning. Unfortunately for him that had been Smallman; he had tried to explain to her that he had got hypothermia, she had misunderstood, congratulated him on locating a statue of an Egyptian goddess, switched off the intercom and the rest, they say, is history. Three fingers lost to frostbite, an inquiry and the end of her career in the museum service.

"What are we to do, sweetkins?"

Ball's voice brought her back to reality.

"The scandal, we shall never get any more inmates, no more wrinklies, no more cash and our dream of a two berth static caravan in Cleethorpes will be nothing more than that, a dream."

"Stop whingeing, Donald, for God's sake" snapped Smallman.

She shocked herself with her sharp, forceful tone, but the thought of losing her dream home was too much to bear.

"Get a grip, man, the publicity might work in our favour, free advertising and the name of Scotswood Manor on everybody's lips. Think about it, anyone wanting to be shot of their geriatric grannies will send them here… far from a disaster, this could be the making of us!"

Ball smiled. *Could this be his Hillary?* he thought as he gazed admiringly across the room at the object of his adoration; this new rather forceful personality made him view her in a totally different and exciting light.

CHAPTER 3

By five o'clock that afternoon Scotswood Manor was returning to what passed as normal. Summoned by the dinner bell, a small crocodile of elderly residents was making its way down the narrow corridor to the dining room.

"It's like the M25 at rush hour," quipped Langton to Clive as they met at the top of the stairs, each unable to reach their destination due to the congested mess of mobility-aided humanity before them.

"Good idea," thought Clive out loud.

"What is?" responded Langton, half-interestedly.

"To have a cull, 'bout time we got rid of some of these, make less work for the both of us!"

Langton was used to Clive's inappropriate humour. She smirked and was about to reply when the conversation was cut short by a series of shouts and the smashing of plates from the room at the end of the corridor.

Clive and Langton looked at one another.

"Looks like Bronwyn's lost the plot again. Someone's objected to her buggered about beef I don't doubt. 'Bout time the old bat retired," mused Clive, but Langton had already seized her chance. Having spotted a gap in the queue she darted off down the hall.

Fricker and O'Brien had set up an incident room in a small annex adjacent to the sun lounge, overlooking the garden.

"Bring them in, one at a time, Constable," yawned Fricker addressing the uniformed officer waiting at the door.

"We'll start with the vicar… what's his name, O'Brien?"

"Donald S Ball, sir, and he is not a vicar."

"Whatever," snapped Fricker. "Let's get on with it, we don't want to be here all night."

Fricker had prepared a list of pertinent questions to ask each of the members of staff and residents, seventy-five in fact, gleaned from his intensive study of old Agatha Christie novels and Inspector Morse videos. This research had, he believed, helped to finely tune his investigational technique and now he finally had the opportunity to put it into practice.

An hour later Ball was still sitting opposite Fricker and O'Brien. He looked tired and a little jaded.

"Question twenty-seven, Mr Ball, what is your mother's maiden name?"

"With all due respect, Inspector, this is not getting us anywhere," he replied.

O'Brien found it hard not to agree, although he kept his thoughts strictly to himself.

"Her name, Mr Ball," repeated Fricker, "or perhaps you never had one?"

O'Brien squirmed in embarrassment and the room descended into silence. After more than a minute Ball stuttered back into life.

"I will not under any circumstances be spoken to like that and I refuse to answer any more of your inane questions," he stated vigorously. Then with a flourish he flung back his chair and stormed out of the room.

O'Brien looked across at his boss and sighed.

"What a wuss, eh Sergeant?" commented Fricker raising his eyebrows.

"A week's wages says he's our man… bring in the next, but it's all academic now."

O'Brien went outside into the sun lounge to where the staff and now fully-fed residents of Scotswood were gathered. They sat clucking away like a gaggle of demented chickens waiting for a handful of corn.

As he surveyed the room he noticed, in the far corner sitting away from the main group, a small clique hunched over an array of coffee cups. They were whispering furtively.

Bronwyn-Jones, Langton and the handyman, Clive; *the three witches*, thought O'Brien as he walked towards their table. Catching sight of his approach their chattering stopped abruptly. As one they all turned to look in his direction.

"Can we help you at all?" asked Langton and Bronwyn-Jones in unison.

"The Inspector would like a word with you. Mrs Langton first and if you don't mind waiting, you next Clive with Mrs Jones straight after," stated O'Brien.

"It's Bronwyn-Jones, see Sergeant," interjected the cook, "but I've a casserole in the oven and I can't let my puddings rise too quickly. Tomorrow's dinner see, I need to be seen first or preferably not at all." Her pleading, however, fell on deaf ears. By the time she had finished her spiel, O'Brien and Langton had already left the room.

"Where were you, Mrs Langton, when the murder took place?" asked Fricker before she had even sat down at the table. *There was no point wasting time, Ball did it, it was so blindingly obvious*, he thought, as he waited for his answer, *that even O'Brien must have realised*.

"I was de-fleeing Otto."

"I realise we live in enlightened times, Mrs Langton … but is that legal?"

"Otto is my Doberman dog, Inspector," she replied with undisguised disdain.

Fricker spluttered slightly, then having dismissed his subconscious vision of woman and dog he moved on. "That will be all, madam, thank you. Bring in the next as you see her out, O'Brien."

By ten in the evening Fricker and O'Brien had run out of steam. They both sat back in the lounge bar of the Reckless Hedgehog reflecting on the day's events. A soft haze of cigar smoke, accompanied by the pungent smell of stale beer and body odour drifted through the air, obscuring the slightly faded red flock wallpaper and nicotine-stained magnolia artex ceiling.

The Hedgehog was Fricker's local and he often enjoyed a gin and tonic there at the end of a day's work.

Tonight was different, however, Fricker was mentally drained; he needed something stronger. The G & T had been sidelined in favour of a port and lemon, which he described to Tony O'Brien as fuel for his brain cells.

O'Brien sat opposite his inspector, supping his pint of the strong local bitter. He smiled to himself and mused that it would take more than a port and lemon to stimulate Fricker's grey matter. The smile turned to a smirk and then a slight chuckle as his imagination added the thought that it would probably need a lobotomy.

He was stirred from his musings by the DI's droning voice. Oblivious to the distracted look on the face of his sergeant, Fricker was relating the story of how early in his career at Hampton le Heath, he had arrested the previous landlord of the Hedgehog for an out-of-date tax disc. This was a story that O'Brien sadly remembered being told on every occasion he had accompanied his superior to the pub.

"How did you think it went today then, sir?" asked O'Brien, in a desperate effort to stem the story's flow.

"Oh today, very sad, how anyone could kill such a poor defenceless old lady. But that aside, em, yes, well you know, it was him, O'Brien, without a shadow of a doubt, it was the vicar."

O'Brien sighed in exasperation. Past experience had showed

him the futility of correcting his superior when he had his one-track mind in gear. Instead he chose to speed up the consumption of his pint and make an excuse to leave.

CHAPTER 4

The next morning a slight rolling mist covered the ground in front of Scotswood Manor.

Through the gloom a few dim lights flickered from the windows of the building and deep inside the dark corridors of the west wing the shrill bell of a telephone broke the sleepy silence.

"You got it wrong, you fool!" snapped the voice at the other end of the line.

"You killed the wrong wrinkly, are you completely brainless?"

"No... no," came the reply, "I did as you told me – batter the bat in flat thirty-two, that's what you said!"

The static on the line hummed, the only sound in a silence that seemed to last for minutes. Then the caller spoke again.

"Flat twenty-three, I told you flat twenty-three. What were you thinking?"

"Oh God, I'm sorry. I'm dyscalculic... I couldn't help it," came the stuttering response.

"I don't care if you're Dick's Aunt Nora... you do the job properly or you'll find yourself the main ingredient of that awful compost you put on your precious roses, understand?"

The phone went dead and a low sobbing sound was all that could be heard in the early morning quiet of the west wing corridor.

"I think we'll make old Ball stew for a while, O'Brien!" stated Fricker as they drove down the Manor's drive. "I suppose we ought to have a word with the other residents. Just to clarify one or two points, but as I said last night, it's cut and dry, the vicar's our man."

O'Brien sat quietly, concentrating on the road before him. Suddenly out of the swirling mist, straight across the road in front of the car came not one, but four elderly residents hunched over tartan shopping trolleys.

The car screeched to a shuddering halt on the loose gravel, narrowly missing the last of the convoy. O'Brien and Fricker looked in disbelief as the figures slowly disappeared, once again enveloped in the gloom.

"What the hell!" shouted O'Brien as he jumped out of the car, followed shortly by his superior. They both stood motionless, speechlessly gazing in the direction the apparitions had gone.

"Inspector Fricker, Sergeant O'Brien!" came a voice from behind. "I'm so sorry."

The forms of Langton and a heavily salivating Otto appeared as if from nowhere.

"Once they start moving the ladies just seem to have tunnel vision," she said.

"What, where, why are they out at this time?" stammered O'Brien as Fricker gazed on in shell-shocked silence.

"Oh, it's," she hesitated, "their morning constitutional, a healthy body, a healthy mind and all that even applies when you are ninety-five. You should try it Sergeant."

Fricker gawped, open-mouthed. Before he could structure a sentence in response, she too had faded away in the general direction of the Manor's garden.

O'Brien broke the silence.

"Very strange, did you notice, sir?"

"What! Notice what?" snapped Fricker tersely.

His short tone confirmed what O'Brien had deduced over the years. DI Fricker was certainly not a morning person.

Disregarding this thought he continued.

"The old dears, sir, they never even glanced in our direction, not even when we nearly hit them, it was as if they were drugged."

"You've been watching too many episodes of *Colombo*, O'Brien. You heard the Langton woman, it was an exercise class; now let's get back to business. I've a vicar to victimise!"

Five minutes later Fricker and O'Brien were sitting opposite Ball in his office, waiting patiently as Smallman nervously poured tea into the cups and saucers laid out on the tray before them.

"I want a full list of all your residents and then I want to interview them one by one, Mr Ball, is that clear?"

"Yes, Inspector," replied Ball. "They've a whist drive this afternoon, followed by an hour of 'sing along with Alan'. Alan Le-Stoppe is our resident volunteer organist. He knows how to murder a song so you might find them slightly comatose after all that. May I suggest you talk to them tomorrow?"

"No, Mr Ball, you may not suggest anything! O'Brien, take WPC Cole, she should be here by now, and Miss Smallman. Change of plan, they should have had breakfast by now so round the inmates up, it will save time if I talk to them en masse."

O'Brien sighed, then, accompanied by Smallman, he left the room.

Fricker turned towards his prime suspect. An undisguised smirk of satisfaction lighting up his face.

"Ok, Mr Ball, I know you did it so let's not waste any time. Answer these questions and I'll go easy on you. Why, when and how, Mr Ball?"

Ball stared straight back across the dusty, dark mahogany tabletop.

Enough was enough. He emitted a loud sigh and summoning all his subdued morsels of confidence addressed his accuser.

"Detective Inspector Fricker, I did not kill Stella Maitland, I had no reason to. She was a paying resident and anyway, I have an alibi."

The silence in the room could have been cut with a knife.

"I was with Hillary when Stella was killed, ask her if you like."

He paused for effect then added, "Now will that be all, Inspector?"

Fricker was visibly taken aback; he had not expected that response. In fact if he were honest, all he had expected was a confession.

"Y... yes," he stammered. Remaining seated he stared, unblinking at the wood-panelled wall as Ball walked out of his office.

Giles Fricker was still staring straight ahead when Constable Rita Cole knocked on the office door.

Rita was twenty-three, slim with dark brown eyes and shoulder-length auburn hair.

"They're ready for you, sir," Cole said as she entered the room.

Cole had long been the unobtainable object of Fricker's pent-up desire and his eyes brightened momentarily as they slowly moved in her direction.

At the same time that Fricker was observing Cole, Cole was observing her superior. She noted that his bottom lip was protruding even further than usual and above, a deep frown burrowed into his forehead. It was clear to her now: he definitely resembled a slightly sad, squashed bullfrog and the reassuring thought resurfaced in her mind that she could never do it with him. Well, unless a promotion depended on it perhaps. Her mind hesitated briefly as it digested the suggestion, then comfortingly rejected the idea out of hand.

"Something amusing you, Cole?"

In an instant she banished the smile from her face. "No, sir" she replied.

Ever changeable, Fricker's thoughts returned to his conversation with Ball.

"Cole," he said, "do I look like a fool?"

"Well, sir," she began.

Almost at once Fricker knew he had made a mistake; he mentally kicked himself. Why hadn't he remembered WPC Cole's almost obsessive interest in the *Oxford English Dictionary*?

"It depends how you look at it, sir," she continued.

"Do you mean a fool, a silly, empty-headed person, dupe or simpleton, jester or clown? Or alternatively, were you referring to a fool, a dessert of pureed fruit mixed with cream?"

Before Fricker could answer Cole continued.

"I could not possibly say, sir, but DS Smithers in vice said, when I met him the other day in the canteen at HQ, that he saw you as a—"

"That's more than enough, Cole!" interjected Fricker, thankful for the opportunity to stem the tide.

"Tell O'Brien that I will be along shortly."

A musty smell of camphor oil and pungent pound shop fragrance pervaded the air of the dining room as Giles Fricker entered through the main door from reception. The twenty-two residents and staff of Scotswood Manor sat in rows facing the small staged area at the end of the room. Most were at least semi-conscious, although from two or three there emanated deep throaty snores, emphasising how oblivious they were to everything around them.

"Uh, um," Fricker cleared his throat. "Thank you ladies and gentlemen, I am—"

"Are you a doctor?" interrupted a blue rinsed, gingham-clad lady who was certainly the wrong side of ninety.

"I wish he were my doctor," she continued, nudging her equally elderly companion and dislodging her bifocals in the process.

Ignoring the interruption he continued, "I am Detective Inspector Fricker. Yesterday, as I'm sure you are aware, Stella Maitland was murdered."

A loud wail boomed out from Martha Nixdorf followed by a cacophony of sighs, scolds and soothing mumblings from those around her. It took a full five minutes for Hillary Smallman and

Margaret Bronwyn-Jones to placate Martha and in the process prevent her from causing actual bodily harm to Edna, who had vigorously expressed her view that "surely she doth protest too much."

By this time Fricker's patience had all but deserted him. He finished the meeting with a short, "If you have any information whatsoever, please let me know," collected his papers and headed for the sanctuary of the outside world.

CHAPTER 5

At one o'clock, after a light lunch, Fricker sat back in his leather armchair, gazing out of the window of his office, his chin resting firmly in his hands. The shrill ring of the telephone abruptly woke him from his morose malaise.

With O'Brien and Cole having left to attend the autopsy on Stella Maitland, Fricker picked up the receiver.

"Hampton le Heath local police unit, Detective Inspector Fricker speaking."

The voice at the other end of the line was quiet and wobbly.

"Inspector, I heard you at, um, the Manor this morning – or was it yesterday – anyway—"

"Yes," interjected Fricker his impatience level already reading six on his irritation scale.

"Oh... I, um, have something to tell you, it's about the garden."

"What do you mean... who is this speaking?"

"Oh, um, it's Connie Fanshaw, oh, someone's coming, I can't speak now." There followed a short silence. Then with two clicks the phone went dead.

The following morning Ball and Smallman were standing outside the blue and white police taped door to flat thirty-two.

"What time is the reporter due, darling?" asked Ball as he gazed vacantly down the empty corridor. "Whoever did this must have either been very lucky not to have been seen or was known to the other residents, don't you think, darling?"

Without waiting for a reply he continued.

"Otherwise someone would have told Fricker that they had seen a stranger."

"Maybe," Smallman replied, "but that's not our problem, is it!"

She glanced at her watch.

"The reporter's due in two minutes. We must remain focused, we need to milk this situation for the maximum publicity as agreed and remember, no crying, Donald, keep a stiff upper lip."

"No, sweetkins, I promise," and stifling a blub or two he set about arranging his face ready for the press.

Twenty minutes later the bell at Scotswood Manor rang. After a moment's delay Smallman drew back the rusty Victorian bolts and opened the door.

Smallman was small, there were few smaller, but by anyone's standards the woman she greeted at the door was minute.

Looking down she addressed her visitor.

"Good morning, I'm Hillary Smallman, Mr Ball's personal assistant and you are?"

"'Ello, so sorry I am late. I am Jessica Garcia Aldoraz Dominguez from the *Evening Argos*. I am, how you say, a reactor."

"A reporter, Miss Dominguez, a reporter," corrected Smallman who was still coming to terms with the sight before her.

"Do follow me."

Jessica Garcia Aldoraz Dominguez was a little less than four foot three. Short, dumpy with legs that made up in width what they lacked in height. She had long straight, highlighted blonde hair. Her face, although generally pleasant to look at, was dominated by a lengthy ski-sloped nose, topped with a prominent kink.

Dominguez was well aware of her shortcomings; but despite everything she believed she had succeeded in life. Having left the small goat farming community in northern Spain where she was raised, she had travelled to England to improve her English, eventually settling in Hampton le Heath where she had landed her job with the local evening paper.

"It is so cold, so very cold," she said as she clambered up the small stone steps and followed Smallman through the reception area into Donald Ball's office.

"That's some weight you're carrying, dear," said Ball as Smallman and her companion entered the room.

Dominguez was taken aback; this tall man, a priest making remarks about her size. Long subdued memories of her childhood church, St Aldegunais and the shadowy figure of Father Alfonso began to surface when, to her relief, realisation suddenly dawned.

"Oh, you mean my bag, sir, my bag. Oh my bag it is so heavy, a very heavy bag, it is so—"

"Yes, we get the point," snapped Smallman.

"May I introduce Miss Dominguez, Donald, the reporter from the *Argos*."

Five minutes later, all three were seated. The heavy bag, now devoid of the large twin spool tape recorder it had contained, was propped up against Dominguez's chair and three steaming cups of tea stood on a tray in the centre of the desk.

"Miss Dominguez, you may ask us anything you wish to know," stated Ball.

"Thank you, Mr Ball, what type of avert are you wanting to have, please?" Before he could reply she continued. "Miss Smallman, she says you want to show Scotswood Manor as, how you say, the place where we take care of your loved ones. Si, is that right?"

"Exactly right, Miss Dominguez," interjected Smallman with a smile, "where we take care of everything."

Back at Hampton le Heath Fricker was standing at the end of the small briefing room, his team seated in front of him viewing an enlarged map of Scotswood Manor.

"Ok team, can someone tell me where we are at this point of time?" began Fricker.

"The briefing room, sir," piped up Constable Day.

"Excellent, Day! Make a note of that, O'Brien – excellent observational skills. Now what about the enquiry… we have a murder scene, a body, a weapon, what more do we need?"

"A cup of tea, sir?" suggested Day.

"That would be nice… and biscuits, Cole, see what you can sort out. You'll go far, Day, if you keep this up. O'Brien, any other ideas?"

Sergeant O'Brien sighed, he should have been used to Fricker's briefings by now, but surely with a murder even Detective Inspector Fricker might have moved up a notch, he thought.

"What about the message you received yesterday, sir?"

"Message, O'Brien? What message was that?"

"From a Connie Fanshaw. About a garden?"

"Ah, yes, that message. Just testing, team. I've thought about that, O'Brien, never heard of the woman and anyway I've got a… minimalist garden, back to nature, that's me, not a dahlia in sight, must have been a wrong number."

"Yes, sir, but—" He stopped. *It wasn't worth the bother*, thought O'Brien who, reining in his increased irritation, tried to move the meeting forward.

"Well, sir, the post mortem revealed what Dr Body suspected, a single blow to the head with no other visible injuries."

"Okay, O'Brien, that's enough of the medical details for now; we're just about to have our tea and biscuits. Cole and myself will return to Scotswood to re-question the vicar. While we're away I suggest you and that smart young man Day, check on our victim's past. See if there are any reasons why the vicar would kill her."

"He's not a vicar, sir, and he has an ali—" O'Brien again stopped in mid-sentence. DI Fricker had already moved on to what he considered to be more important matters.

"Jammy Dodger or shortbread, Cole, what do you think?"

It was all too much for O'Brien. Increasingly exasperated, he grabbed Day by the collar and frog-marched him out of the room.

"But my tea, Sarge," protested the young constable as he was swiftly moved into the sergeant's office and deposited behind a desk.

"Look, smart arse, you might be the inspector's 'Blue Eyed Boy' but to me you're nothing but a jug-eared half-wit with less grey matter than a decomposing mullet. Get on your computer and find out all you can about Connie Fanshaw and Scotswood Manor."

"But, Sergeant, the DI said—" protested Day.

"Bugger the inspector!"

Day's eyes lit up at the thought. O'Brien continued.

"If we're going to solve this crime, those of us who have brains better start using them. The plods can research Ms Maitland; we've got to think outside the box."

Giles Fricker was happy as he sat beside WPC Cole en route to Scotswood Manor. All was well in his world, a major crime nearly solved and he, Detective Inspector Giles Fricker, was obviously idolised by this young attractive WPC. She surely must have realised by now what a catch he was, if not, then it would be rude not to tell her. After all once everything had been sorted out, a significant promotion was in the pipeline. Maybe, he mused, Fricker of the Yard.

"Cole, or may I call you Rita?"

He continued without waiting for a reply.

"Rita, as I am sure you have noticed over recent months—"

WPC Cole's grip on the steering wheel tightened and a thin bead of perspiration trickled down her brow.

"Noticed what in particular, sir?" she asked, her voice trembling slightly as she noticed droplets of saliva ooze from the corners of his frantically wobbling bottom lip.

"Oh Rita," Fricker continued. "Rita, I'm a man in love! And the object of my desire is—"

He hesitated nervously and yet again it was too late.

Fricker quickly realised the error he had made. The moment's hesitation had left the gate ajar and Rita Cole grasped the opportunity with eager relief.

"I take it, sir, that you mean by 'object', your victim or target and by alluding to your victim as one, whom you desire or yearn for, as though in love, you actually mean you prize him. Therefore you are in reality expressing, if you don't mind me saying, sir, in a slightly clumsy way that you are desperate to nail the vicar for his alleged crime. Is that so, sir?"

Fricker sighed and pouted despondently as the moment dissolved under the barrage of words.

"Uh, yes, WPC Cole, that must be the case," he stated. His mind lapsing into a deep melancholic malaise as they continued their journey in subdued silence.

CHAPTER 6

Subdued silence was also the order of the day in Sergeant O'Brien's office as he and Day sat, absorbed at their computers.

Day; his mother, desperate for a girl and obsessed with an American actress named Doris, had, in her disappointment, christened him Dorian.

His formative years had been spent in pursuits often reserved for the fairer sex. Not that there was anything wrong with cross-stitch, Barbies and pressed flowers. In fact the latter had made the rough games of rugby, played at secondary school, a lot more interesting. Despatched to the wing, Dorian had spent more of his time picking flowers on the touchline than running with the ball. Sadly, however, his genteel manner was cause for ridicule and bullying by the majority of his peers and in an effort to toughen his son up, Dorian's father, a fan of Jack Warner and *The Blue Lamp*, had persuaded his wife that a life in the force would be the making of their son. As a result, Day found himself at Police Training College and subsequently behind a desk at Hampton le Heath.

It wasn't all bad, he thought, with shifts he had time to indulge his hobbies and as this was a small station with only a few staff he managed to get by without too much abuse.

Then of course there was Detective Inspector Giles Fricker. *What a man*, thought Day, a true leader of men and the object of his adoration.

"Day, dreaming again, are you?" boomed the still seething O'Brien.

"Oh no, Sarge, I'm concentrating on the task in hand," stammered Day as he hastily removed a Flower Show web page from his screen.

"What have you found out about this Fanshaw woman?"

"Well, Sergeant, very little I'm afraid. The only reference to Fanshaw in Hampton le Heath goes back to 1672 when Sir Charles Fanshaw was a well-known country gentleman and Member of Parliament. When he died suddenly in 1697 the family seems to go off the radar."

"Well, keep digging, Day, and don't forget, I want a full report on Scotswood Manor as well. There's a reason behind the Maitland woman's death and we're going to find out what it is!"

Connie Fanshaw had been a resident of Scotswood Manor for four years. Like the majority of the other elderly people who resided in this abode she was an ex-teacher. A pianist of some note she had taught at primary school level and then as a private piano teacher for many years.

Her family had once been great landowners in the locality until her great, great, great grandfather died and to her family's shame his philandering ways had come to light.

Sir Charles, it appeared, had been fond of the 'sins of the flesh'. A dabbler with the local damsels he had a particular interest in the parson's daughter. A matter, that on its own would not, in those times, have been too much of a cause for concern, had it not been for the fact that sadly his lust had not just been satiated with the daughter. To the eternal shame of the Fanshaw family, not only the daughter but also the wife and sadly the parson himself had been defrocked within the walls of the family home. In addition the fate of Bruno, the elderly family retainer, was deemed too distasteful for even the good burghers of Hampton le Heath to record in their journals. Once Sir Charles had died, the family's secret was revealed and there followed years of disgrace and ruin as the Fanshaw name became synonymous with vile debauchery.

By the time Connie Fanshaw was ushered into the world in 1927, much water had gone under the bridge. Although no longer Lords of the Manor the Fanshaws had regained a reasonable standing in the community. Through a few cleverly calculated marriages the family fortune had started to re-grow.

Connie, the only surviving daughter, had few relatives. Her sister had died in childbirth and aunts and uncles had passed on over time. Now only two other members of the family, as far as she was aware, were left alive. There was Cousin Martha, an aging non-conformist missionary, who at sixty-three had left England to indoctrinate the river tribes of Papua New Guinea with biblical tales. After monthly letters for the first six years she had not been heard of since. That was in 1995, although in the current March issue of *Missionary News*, Connie had seen a reference to a Sister Martha and her rather inappropriate relationship with a tribal elder, so perhaps, she had mused, the Fanshaw genes had re-surfaced after all these years. *Although*, thought Connie when she had read this, *there may be more than one Sister Martha in New Guinea and more than likely her Martha had ended up in a pot like so many who had gone before her.*

The other remaining Fanshaw was her niece, Pauline Petrie, who lived less than seven miles from Scotswood Manor. Pauline was a bit of a glamour puss, a facet of her personality that did not quite fit in with her nine-to-five role as a bank teller. Pauline loved to spend her money and in particular other people's money. She had, over the years, worked her way through many a boyfriend's wallet before moving on to the next one and Connie had not seen her niece for a good three months. Not that this bothered Connie.

The last visit had caused chaos as Pauline, or rather, the mutton dressed as lamb with a cleavage of astronomical proportions, had paraded through Scotswood Manor in a denim mini skirt that left nothing to the imagination. Four of the male residents including Mr Le-Stoppe, the organist, had to be treated with oxygen by paramedics. In addition Mr Delve and Fondle, as he was jokingly known by the female residents, a Portuguese ex-opera singer from flat sixty-seven, had been in intensive care ever since.

"No, she's better off keeping away," thought Connie out loud as she sat pondering over the vagaries of her remaining relatives.

On her desk lay a partially completed letter to DI Fricker. She had decided to write to the inspector after her telephone call had been abruptly cut short by the arrival of the cook and the lunchtime trolley. *A letter was*, she thought, *probably the best way of alerting the police to what was really going on at Scotswood Manor. After all, the nice Mr Fricker had said, "if there was anything you knew, then please get in touch."*

She had just settled down to continue writing, when her concentration was yet again interrupted by, on this occasion, the shrill ring of her telephone on the desk beside her.

"Hello, Connie Fanshaw speaking," she answered. "Who is that please?" she continued.

The voice on the other end of the line seemed familiar, but slightly muffled.

"I need to see you urgently, Connie, meet me in the garden in five minutes."

Connie still struggled to identify the caller and asked again.

"Sorry, who is that please? I can't make out your voice."

"Five minutes in the garden, Connie," came the reply and the line went dead.

How strange, she thought; but as Connie had always been an inquisitive person she got up and prepared to go out.

Fifteen minutes after Connie Fanshaw left her flat, DI Fricker and WPC Cole left the main reception of the Manor.

"Well, he did it, Cole, whatever he says he did it," whined Fricker.

"But he has an alibi, sir, Miss Smallman openly states that she was with him for the duration of the time in question," replied Cole.

"Yes, that may be so, but I know the vicar did it. That, Cole, is why I'm a Detective Inspector. Isn't it?"

"Yes, sir, I'm sure that's why you're a Detective Inspector," replied Cole in an ever more resigned tone that was completely lost on Fricker. His mind had already moved on.

"Cole, would you like to go for a drink?"

"No thank you, sir," she replied. "Should we not go back to work? It is only two o'clock and we do have a murder to solve, sir."

"You're quite right Cole, you are always so right. Let's take a rain check, perhaps later, Rita?"

"No thank you, sir, I'm washing my hair."

She opened the car door for her superior who, lip pouting in an expression of hopeless despair, climbed into the passenger seat.

The scream reached Fricker and Cole as they drove, windows open, out of the gates of Scotswood Manor. At the same time the sound so surprised Edna and Hilda that they rose out of their armchairs, scrabble letters cascading into the air, their hands above their heads in alarm.

"Goodness gracious, old girl," exclaimed Hilda. "That was a top—"

"Don't start, Hilda!" interrupted Edna with venom. "You said that last time and you were wrong, you're always wrong so don't try being right, it does not work, dear. Mind you," continued Edna, "there was a small twinge of soprano there, I have to admit. Crossed with, strangely I may say, a hint of baritone I feel."

Having abandoned the car, Cole ran back down the drive and raced around the corner of the west wing. The heavily huffing Fricker followed her at a distance. Stretched out in front of her was the lawn and beyond, the garden and fruit orchard.

A figure stood immobile at the far edge of the grass, a strange wail emanating from her mouth as she stared towards a clump of fruit trees to the left of the vegetable patch.

Fricker caught up with Cole as she came alongside the apron-clad figure of Margaret Bronwyn-Jones.

"Can't you see it?" the cook wailed.

"What?" replied Cole. "Oh that, it's a James Grieve, isn't it?"

"Not the apple tree, stu-pid," Bronwyn-Jones rasped, "that, that thing."

Cole vomited vigorously as she took in the sight before her.

Hanging from the branches of an elderly pear tree, suspended by two blue and white catering apron ties, was the disembowelled body of a mature woman. Her eyes seemed to bulge in terror although, overall, her face had a look of slight surprise as she swayed gently in the early afternoon breeze.

"That's some scarecrow," said Fricker ignoring the sickly green figure of Cole, who now was redecorating the rose bed.

"That is not a scarecrow, Inspector, that's Connie Fanshaw," replied a now slightly more composed Bronwyn-Jones.

They both stood, staring in silence at Connie Fanshaw. Her entrails, already the source of interest to a small swarm of flies, hung down likes a ring of Cumberland sausages.

Just as WPC Cole, having recovered some of her equilibrium, joined the two onlookers, the wind wafted a putrid stench in their direction and she jettisoned what remained of her breakfast cereal all over her superior's brushed suede shoes.

"Cole," barked Fricker as he danced backwards in a vain attempt to dodge the final flurry of soggy wheat.

"Cole, call O'Brien and Dr Body, get them here now and make sure nobody enters this area of the garden."

"Yes, sir," spluttered the WPC who quickly turned away and proceeded to make the call.

Fricker also moved away from the grisly scene, beckoning, as he went, to Bronwyn-Jones who had remained transfixed at the image before her.

Having moved to a bench a little further along the left-hand side of the lawn, Fricker began to question his witness.

"So, Mrs Bronwyn-Jones," he began as the formerly subdued feelings of shock started to pulse through his head.

"Tell me what happened, how did you come across the deceased, Connie Fanshaw?"

Bronwyn-Jones, who had continued to regain her composure, began to tell her tale.

"Well Inspector, it was like this see! I was out in the garden, putting my peelings in the com—"

"Sir, sir!" bellowed Cole interrupting the cook in full flow "I've found it, sir!"

"What have you found, Cole? Spit it out," snapped Fricker who then realised that "spit it out" was perhaps not the most appropriate comment bearing in mind Cole's recent state of health.

Still slightly green in the face, WPC Cole stumbled up to her superior. In her hand, it's handle covered in a blue-green nappy sack, was a long bladed knife, the blood that covered its length only just starting to congeal.

"Good God, Cole! Well done, where did you find that?" exclaimed Fricker turning his back on Bronwyn-Jones.

"Behind the wall, sir, near the compost heap," replied the obviously elated WPC, whose more than ample bosom began to swell with pride.

"Ugh, who would leave a nappy bag there?" asked Fricker, not oblivious to the distraction before him.

"No, sir, the knife was behind the wall, the bag was mine."

"I, I did not know that you had a child, Cole," stated Fricker, the disappointment evident in his voice.

"No, sir," Cole blurted out in exasperation. "I carry these bags always, for dog walking, sir, they're ideal."

"Excuse me!" The gruff voice of Bronwyn-Jones brought them both back on track.

"Can I go now, Detective Inspector? I've a plum duff in the oven and if I'm not careful it will sink."

"Ah, um, yes, for the moment, but I might like to speak to you later, Mrs Bronwyn-Jones."

With that the cook strode purposefully off across the lawn.

Seconds later Sergeant O'Brien, PC Day and Dr Body came into view around the corner of the Manor. An ambulance trundled slowly after them, marking its progress across the grass with two brown ruts.

Fricker took O'Brien to one side, Dr Body began to examine the still swaying corpse and Cole set about reviving the prone figure of PC Day who, having taken one look at Connie Fanshaw's earthly remains, fell poleaxed onto the soft grass.

"O'Brien," began an agitated Fricker. "I've interviewed the poor cook, Bronwyn-Jones, she found the body, knows nothing. You better get hold of the vicar, find out where he was this morning and then set about looking for witnesses. Cole has found a knife, could be the weapon, send it for the usual tests, I'm going back to the station, I, I need a rest."

"The cook, sir," replied O'Brien to his already retreating superior. "Did she say why she was out here in the garden?"

"Oh yes, sort of, something about peelings I think, but don't worry, it was the vicar," shouted Fricker as he quickly disappeared out of view.

Giles Fricker's office was in darkness as he dialled the now all too familiar number. There was a short delay before an educated Germanic voice at the other end of the line answered.

"Hello, Doctor Franz-Joseph Schruff, who is this speaking please?"

"It's me Doctor S," came the faint response.

"Now listen to me carefully, I am a psychiatrist not a psychic so please, who is it speaking please?"

"It is me Doctor S, Fricker, I need to talk."

"Ah Fricker, why didn't you say, are you," the doctor hesitated, "are you under the desk again Giles?"

"Yes, Doctor, I am," replied the quiet, almost childlike voice.

He was sitting hunched up in the dark confines of the footwell under the sturdy piece of solid oak furniture. The phone line stretched to breaking point as it strained to reach him in his sanctuary.

"So Giles," continued the doctor. "A bad day at the office I presume?"

Dr Schruff had been Fricker's mentor and confidant ever since the 'flashing vicar' incident. It was then that the powers that be at County HQ decided, having finally found the Detective Inspector in a state of uncontrollable gibbering underneath his desk, that he should seek professional help. Since that time Fricker had, on a number of occasions, made a call to Dr S. As a result the psychiatrist was now beginning to develop a little understanding of his patient's needs.

"Giles!" Dr Schruff reiterated. "We will not get very far if you do not speak to me, will we?"

There was a pause and then the faint voice responded.

"Yes Dr S, a bad week, two murders and I know the vicar did them and—"

"Who, Giles? The flashing vicar did you say, you mean he's back on the scene?"

"No, Doctor," continued Fricker. "A new vicar, he runs the home where the women were murdered. He says he didn't, couldn't have done it, but I know for certain he did and worse still—"

"Another murder!" interrupted the doctor.

"No worse, much worse, I'm in love with a girl, but she doesn't care."

The doctor listened as the voice at the other end of the line dissolved into a series of muffled sobs, which seemed to echo within the dark confines of the oak desk's footwell.

After what seemed an age the sobs subsided. Doctor Schruff cleared his throat and, before his client could introduce any additional details, he began to address what he saw as the root of the problem.

"I believe, having listened to everything you have said, that it is obvious you have a vicar fixation, which is, or has been greatly influenced by your childhood experiences and in particular your relationship with someone very close to you. Was your father a clergyman, Giles?"

"How did you know, doctor?" came the muffled reply. "Although my father was not a vicar, he had connections with the church when I was young, he was," Fricker hesitated.

"Come on, Giles, you can tell me, tell your old friend Doctor Schruff."

"He was, he was," Fricker again hesitated and the sobs returned.

"Giles!" snapped the psychiatrist. He then stopped instantly, realising that perhaps he had been a little sharp. After a short pause he continued in a more conciliatory tone.

"Giles, please tell me what your father was?"

"My father," Fricker squirmed in his cramped sanctuary, struggling to talk. Moments passed, then with an explosion of pent-up anguish he divulged the secret that had haunted him for most of his adult life.

"My father was a… campanologist!"

"Hells bells!" exclaimed the doctor. "No wonder you're so screwed up, Giles. A campanologist, how could he have been so cruel?"

With that, the sobbing returned at the other end of the line.

Ignoring the obvious discomfort of his client, Doctor Schruff continued his deliberations.

"This woman, Giles, the one with whom you are, you say, in love with, is she aware of your feelings?"

"I don't know, I've tried to tell her, but she just doesn't seem to want to know," replied a disconsolate Fricker.

"And is she too a campanologist?" continued the doctor. "Whatever," he went on without waiting for a reply, "either way you need to tackle these demons face on, Giles, remember what we discussed the last time you rang?"

"Yes, Doctor Schruff, I do."

"Then you still carry the severed rabbit's foot and putrefied Bockwurst sausage?"

"Yes, Doctor Schruff, I still carry them," said Fricker, his mood now beginning to sound a little brighter.

"Then get up now, SCHNELL! Stop whingeing under the desk, dummkopf. Those two items are all you need to see you through your darkest hour. How do you think that great man G W Brush managed to make all of his marvellous decisions? He travelled nowhere without his seven-year-old hamburger with extra relish."

"I do understand what you are saying, Doctor," responded Fricker as he crawled out from under his desk.

"However, I think we need to talk some more about your father, Giles. A campanologist, how disgusting, it should not be legal. Ring me next week," the doctor stated then hung up.

Fricker sat down on the edge of his desk, his mind in turmoil as he tried to understand the week's events, the doctor's advice and the baggage that haunted the inner recesses of his mind. *The doctor was right*, reflected Fricker as his hand delved into the inner breast pocket of his jacket and withdrew a sealed plastic bag containing his two lucky charms. *I need to focus*, he thought as he gave the package an affectionate squeeze. Placing it on his desk, he leaned across, switched on the office light and set about listing his ideas.

CHAPTER 7

The following morning, the sun shone brightly down on the lawn at Scotswood Manor, which was now a hive of activity. White-suited Scene of Crime Officers moved in and out of the blue and white tent that covered the area where Connie Fanshaw's body had been found. Sergeant O'Brien shouted instructions to a variety of officers who had been seconded to assist the small team at Hampton le Heath. A gaggle of residents formed at the edge of the gravel drive that surrounded the lawn to watch the proceedings with ghoulish interest and a little concern.

"Cole, Day!" bellowed O'Brien. The two PCs stopped dead in their tracks as they walked along the edge of the vegetable garden. They turned abruptly, quickened their pace and were soon standing beside their sergeant.

"I want you both to go and have a good trawl through Fanshaw's rooms, find out everything you can about the woman and look for anything that might give us a clue as to why she was killed," instructed O'Brien.

"Yes, Sarge," replied Cole. "Do you know which was her flat, Sarge?"

"No, ask Mr Ball and when you do send him over here, the DI wants me to have yet another word with him so I'd best get it over with. Oh and don't forget to blue tape the doorway when you finish."

As the PCs entered the Manor they veered left off the main entrance hall and Day knocked tentatively on the sturdy door to Ball's office.

"Yes, do come in," came the response. With that the two officers made their way into the room.

Ball sat slumped behind his desk, a large pile of paperwork accumulated in front of him. "Mr Ball," began Cole. "Could you tell me what was Connie Fanshaw's flat number? We need her key, if you don't mind."

"Er, yes, Officer, it's all so very sad, Connie wouldn't have hurt a fly, such a lovely old lady. Have you any idea who could have done this awful deed?" asked Ball.

"No, sir, I'm afraid not, but our superior wishes to talk to you, so if you have any questions please refer them to him, he is on the lawn if you would be so kind as to join him, sir," replied Cole.

Ball looked taken aback and the slight colour he had visibly drained from his thin face.

"Oh my God, not Inspector Fricker, not again. I've already told him I did not do it, I've an alibi, this is persecution!" Ball wailed.

Cole interjected to save any further distress and stop his whining.

"No, sir, it's Sergeant O'Brien who would like to talk to you. The flat number if you please."

"Oh thank God, number twenty-three, the key is on the left hand hook, second row on your right as you go out," replied Ball who got up from his seat and proceeded to follow the two officers as they left his office.

Day and Cole passed the door to flat thirty-two, glancing as they did to check that the police tape that sealed the entrance was still intact.

They came to a halt outside flat twenty-three.

"What a pleasant shade of pink, don't you think, Rita?" asked Day.

Rita Cole inwardly grimaced. *Why don't they make manly men anymore? What with Fricker and Day there's no hope*, she thought.

"Lovely, dear," she answered with a slight hint of sarcasm. Inserting the key in the door she turned the lock and they both entered the dark hallway.

"You take the bedroom and I'll check the lounge and bathroom," instructed Cole as she strode purposefully into the still curtained front room.

Ignoring the ohs and ahs that emanated from the bedroom as PC Day took in the chintz décor, WPC Cole surveyed the lounge. Peeking out through a gap in the curtains was a sturdy tripod mounted telescope. The area around it revealed a small mahogany occasional table on which lay a half-open notebook. Cole picked up the book and on closer inspection observed a series of dated entries that appeared to give details of visits to the garden by a wide assortment of people over the last two to three months. Following procedure she securely bagged the evidence.

Having opened the curtains she continued to work her way through the room paying particular attention to a mound of papers on Connie Fanshaw's desk.

Her deliberations were cut short by a cry of "Rita!" from the bedroom. Thinking the worst Cole turned and raced into the hallway only to crash headlong into Day. They both went sprawling over, taking with them, in a tangle of limbs, an ornate reproduction Chinese vase. The two officers came to rest in a heap of shattered china against the kitchen doorframe.

"Oh! Rita, you are very vigorous," spluttered Day as he endeavoured to extract himself from beneath his colleague.

"What the, why did you call out, you idiot? I thought you were in trouble," rasped Cole who by now had clambered to her feet and was brushing off the fragments of pot from her creased uniform.

"There's no need for sharp words," bleated Day. "I only wanted to show you this," producing, as he spoke, a slightly faded photograph of a relatively young woman and an older-looking man standing in front of what looked like the entrance to a nightclub.

"So, what's so special about that?" snapped Cole, whose anger was, if anything, rising by the second.

"Well," continued Day, "on the back of the photo someone, presumably Connie, has written 'niece Pauline and friend outside the Fantasy Club'."

"So," interrupted Cole. "She's got a niece. Fine, bag it with the rest of the evidence."

"No, Rita, look at the man friend, who does it remind you of?"

"Uh, he's blooming ugly that's for sure. I don't know, who?"

Day grinned from ear to ear. "Look again, if he wasn't dressed as a man I would be certain that the man was the cook! Margaret Bronwyn-Jones."

"You're right, Day," responded Cole, "but there is only one flaw in your argument. Bronwyn-Jones is a woman."

"Yes, I see your point," conceded Day as he proceeded to file his find, but he added, "I've an eye for these things, Rita, you mark my words there's more to this than meets the eye."

"Well, you can ask Margaret if she's really a Martin when you next see her," called Cole as she disappeared back into the lounge to continue her search of the desk.

Within twenty minutes both officers had completed their work. The only addition to their bag of evidence being a half-finished letter to Inspector Fricker, which at first glance seemed, thought Cole, to outline some of the points made in the notebook she had found earlier. *That's the trouble with the retired*, thought Cole, *nothing better to do than spy on their neighbours. As a result any insignificant happening seems to be blown out of all proportion.*

As Day and Cole left flat twenty-three they sealed the door with blue and white tape and made their way onto the lawn to catch up with Sergeant O'Brien.

CHAPTER 8

The thin ray of sunlight lit up the stairwell as Fricker bounded, two steps at a time, down from his office to the custody suite. All was well in his world. Following his talk with Doctor Schruff and after a good night's sleep Fricker had never felt better.

"Good morning, Robson," he bellowed as he rounded the corner into the small, dark reception area.

"Oh, good, good morning, sir," blurted out the short, rotund custody sergeant as he quickly stashed a copy of a newspaper under the desk.

"So Robson, how are things this morning? I was—"

Fricker was cut off in mid-sentence by a furious banging at the front door that almost made it fly off its hinges. Both officers gazed open mouthed as the large oak door flexed violently under the assault from outside.

"Oh I'm sorry, sir," stammered Robson. "I must have left the 'out for lunch sign' on yesterday, I'll just undo the latch, sir."

"Don't worry, I'll get it," said Fricker who was already turning the bolt. With one final twist the door flew open and both he and their vigorous visitor tumbled to the ground in a heap of flailing arms and legs.

"Good God, mummy!" exclaimed Fricker who by now was lying prone on the cold tile floor. He stared up into the large expanse of lycra-clad bosom that had enveloped him.

At that very moment there was a bright flash of light from the vicinity of the open doorway.

45

"Who the, what the, get this pervert off me!" shrieked the woman as she struggled to free her arms. Seconds later, having recovered her senses and mobility, she leant back and landed a perfect upper cut to the DI's quivering lower lip.

As Fricker descended into a state of peaceful oblivion the last image he saw was that of a small, hideous creature pointing a camera in the direction of the two intertwined bodies.

Four minutes later, Robson finally managed to extract his inspector from a barrage of further blows delivered by his assailant. When he came round, Fricker found himself sitting in a hard wooden chair gingerly clasping a bag of cold sandwiches from the office fridge to his bruised and swollen face.

"Are you alright, Inspector?" asked a voice that was, thought Fricker, almost sweet, even angel-like.

"Am I dead?" he asked himself out loud. "Is that, is that you, Auntie?"

A short silence ensued and then through the swirling fog that seemed to cover his brain he heard it again.

"I'm so sorry, I didn't mean to hit you so hard, I thought you were a weirdo, I mean you read so much in the papers, don't you?"

Another minute passed and Fricker carefully opened his eyes. Hoping, even expecting to see a pure vision of loveliness before him.

"Aggh!" he exclaimed dropping the sandwich bag to the floor as he stared into the crusty, wizened face of Sergeant Robson.

"I've got you a nice cup of tea, four sugars, sir, just as you like it."

"Where is the woman, Robson?"

"Which one, sir? You do seem to be very popular with the ladies today."

"What are you talking about, man?" snapped Fricker. "The woman who attacked me, where is she?"

"Oh, her, sir, she's just gone to, you know, sir, powder her nose I believe is the expression. But the other lady who came to speak to you—"

"The short ugly one in the doorway?"

"Well you might think that, sir, but I thought she had a hint of Latin charm myself, reminded me of a girl I once knew in the war, met her in a bomb shelter in Clapham. Mind you it was dark, the blackouts you see, sir."

"Shut up, Robson! Who was she?"

"Oh, I'm sorry, she left a card."

Robson passed Fricker a small brightly coloured business card, which read Jessica Garcia Aldoraz Dominguez: reporter with the *Evening Argos*.

"Great that's all we need, the press! What did she say to you before she left, Robson?"

"Well, sir, after she asked to see you, I pointed you out, well the best I could, bearing in mind you were under the other woman at the time. She said, she could see you were busy and she would speak to you some other time, least I think that's what she said, her being Spanish or Chilean or Portuguese or…"

Fricker had already switched off and was staring, despairingly into his hands when he again heard the angelic voice.

"Are you okay now, Inspector?"

Fricker looked up. Before him stood a blonde, statuesque woman of about thirty years of age. She was wearing a short beige mini skirt and a low cut lycra top that barely concealed the enormous cleavage with which Fricker had only too recently become intimately acquainted.

"Inspector Fricker, I'm Pauline Petrie, you left me a message to get in touch? Something about my aunt, Connie Fanshaw?"

If Giles Fricker's jaw could have dropped any further it would have reached the floor.

"You, you had better come to my office, Ms Petrie," he stuttered and with a reluctant step he slowly led the way up the stairs.

Fricker was amazed that one person could get through so many tissues so quickly. Yes, he had just told her that her aunt had been found disembowelled hanging from a fruit tree, but even so, there was a limit. *In addition*, Fricker thought, *there was also the planet to consider*, as his gaze fluctuated between the remnants of a small forest littering his office floor and, across the desk, the twin peaks that dominated his view.

"So Inspector, you are certain that you won't be pressing charges against me?"

Fricker looked confused.

"For my actions earlier. It was a genuine mistake."

"Yes, Ms Petrie, the only thing I shall be pressing," he muttered before re-focusing his mind and continuing. "You can rest assured that our sole concern is to catch your aunt's killer. If you have any other matters you need to discuss with me or anything you need to get off your chest, uh, so to speak, you can ring me on this number." He passed her his card whilst consciously averting his eyes towards the local area map on the far office wall.

"Oh and do call me Giles," he added as a hopeful afterthought.

"Thank you, Giles, you have been so kind and understanding," she said, her voice faltering as Fricker yet again passed her a handful of tissues.

"You must call me Pauline."

He stood up and offered her his hand. As she leaned forward to reach the short way across the desk, Fricker was once again distracted by the heaving mass of curvaceous flesh that was suddenly revealed.

He stumbled forward pulling Pauline's hand vigorously down onto the desk. The intertwined fingers landed with vigour crushing the small plastic bag that lay below. In an instant its sticky, putrefied contents were ejected with such force that they hit the now off balance Pauline Petrie straight between the eyes.

"What the hell is that?" she cried as she franticly tried to remove the pungent mass from her face. She looked down, took one glance at the severed rabbit's foot that lay in her hand, let out an enormous scream and threw the offending object to the floor.

Fricker, now out of tissues, tried desperately to offer words of comfort. They were, however all in vain. His 'angel', uttering every expletive known to man, raced out of the room and descended the stairs. She just managed to avoid a collision with Sergeant O'Brien, WPC Cole and PC Day as they raced up in the opposite direction, before disappearing out of the station door.

"Bloody hell, sir, who was that tart?" exclaimed O'Brien as he walked into the office. "I haven't heard swearing like that since I was in the Paras. Sir?" he hesitated as his eyes scanned the apparently empty room. "Are you there, sir?"

"Um," came the muffled response.

"I think he's under there, Sarge," whispered Day as he pointed to the trailing telephone wire that disappeared over the far edge of the desk.

"What the heck is that smell, sir?" added Cole as the rancid aroma of decaying meat caught her nostrils. It was, however, too much for Day. As he took in the dreadful stench he quickly began to turn a sickly shade of pale cream.

"Oh, it's you, O'Brien, I was just searching for this," said Fricker as first his head and then his arms appeared, followed by his right hand, brandishing the severed rabbit's foot like a trophy.

There was a loud thud from behind O'Brien. He turned just in time to see Day fall to the floor like a thin sapling, narrowly missing the filing cabinet and half-open door as he went.

"She, I mean Pauline must have dropped it as she left. Oh and no, O'Brien she is not a tart. She is the deceased's niece," continued Fricker who by now was slowly rediscovering his equilibrium.

"Of whom, sir, Stella Maitland?" asked Cole.

"No, Cole, she, Pauline Petrie is the niece of Connie Fanshaw."

"Ah yes, sir, of course, we found a picture of her and another person in Connie's room. Doris, I mean Dorian had an idea. He thought he saw someone he knew in the picture, sir."

"Well, Day, come on lad pull yourself together, boy! Tell the Detective Inspector who you saw," boomed O'Brien.

"I think he's not quite with us at the moment, sir," added Cole who by now had bent down beside Day's inert body and was vigorously slapping his face. Fricker slumped back in his chair, rescued the telephone from the floor and quickly, drowning out a distant "Ya, this is Dr Schruff, who is it calling?" replaced the receiver. As he did he surreptitiously scanned the desk for the remaining item from his bag.

"O'Brien, don't worry about Day we'll leave Cole to attend to him, but be a little more gentle with him, Rita."

"So, um, tell me; how are the enquires going? Have we got enough evidence to arrest the vic—"

"No, sir," interrupted O'Brien with such forcefulness that Fricker jumped in his seat.

"Mr Ball could not possibly have committed the murder, the interim autopsy report shows that Connie Fanshaw had been dead only a couple of minutes before we found her and Ball has a cast iron alibi for the time in question."

"Oh yes," interjected Fricker with a sneer. "Just like the Maitland case I assume. What cock and bull story has he come up with this time? Pulled the wool over your eyes, eh, O'Brien?"

"Not quite, sir. You see, at the time of the murder, he was sitting in his office," he said pausing for effect.

"Yes?"

"Being interviewed by WPC Cole and you, sir!"

A bad day had just got worse. Fricker felt his mouth drop open like a trout out of water. He gazed across the room towards where O'Brien and Cole and a now revived PC Day stood.

"Oh," stammered Fricker after what seemed like an eternity of silence. "Ha, have we got any other leads to go on?"

He slumped even further down into his chair and stared at his colleagues with sad, almost pleading eyes.

Despite his tough external shell and regular irritation with his superior's strange obsessions, O'Brien felt a small pang of pity for the dribbling shadow of a man who sat before them.

"Well, sir," began O'Brien in a more comforting tone. "We have the knife that WPC Cole found in the garden. It is still undergoing tests in the lab. Also when Cole and Day were searching Connie Fanshaw's flat they found a letter addressed to you, sir."

"Should I read it, sir?" interjected Cole who had also noticed the look of total despondency that had enveloped her superior's face.

"Uh, um, er, go on, Cole," grunted Fricker.

"Well, sir, it has not been finished, but this is what it says:

'Dear Inspector Fricker, I am sorry for writing, but I had tried to ring you the other day, after your visit to the home and that wonderful speech you made asking for information. But as I'm sure you remember my call was cut short. I'm sorry about that, but the cook arrived with the lunch trolley and she does not like to be kept waiting. She was a bit cross when she found me on the phone, even when I told her it was you I was speaking to. She was quite sharp. Anyway I thought I must tell you about what I saw take place on the lawn, it has happened a few times, always in the morning at about seven o'clock, they are there digging away, I've knocked on the window, but they don't hear me, they are a bit like, you know, as if in a horror movie, like zombies, that's it zombies then off they go and she's always there too. Oh and then of course there's that funny thing going on in the house, always whispering, plotting they are and since poor Stella was murdered well it's all got worse. You need to talk to...' Then it finishes, sir."

"Interesting, sir, this ties in with what we witnessed on our way to Scotswood the other morning," stated O'Brien.

Cole then continued.

"But she leaves a few questions unanswered, sir. In addition as I mentioned earlier, Day found a photograph."

"Tell the Chief Inspector what you saw, Day," snapped O'Brien.

Day, who by now had regained some of his colour, was standing propped up against the filing cabinet. He fumbled about in the evidence bag that had been passed to him by Cole and drew out the faded picture from flat twenty-three. "Sir," he said hesitantly.

"On the back it reads 'niece Pauline and friend outside the Fantasy Club', sir."

"Well, sir," interjected O'Brien. "You can't fail to recognise the tart, but take a close look at the other one, who does that remind you of, sir?"

Fricker peered across at the picture that Day had passed to him and studied the faces. Yes, O'Brien was right, you could not fail to recognise Pauline Petrie, but the other one, the man.

"I'm not sure, O'Brien, but he's certainly ugly."

"Exactly, sir, who's the ugliest person you have seen recently, sir?"

"I'm, there have been a few, someone at Scotswood?"

"Yes, sir," shouted an elated Day. "Margaret Bronwyn-Jones, that's who he is, don't you agree, sir?"

"Good grief, Day," exclaimed Fricker, casting off his melancholy mood in an instant. "You're right, it is Bronwyn-Jones, is that a crime, O'Brien?"

"It should be, sir, it was in the army, at least unofficially, although I did know a couple of women in the Catering Corps who were at least the same size and shape of a man and could very well have been."

"Actually, sir," interrupted Cole, "the correct term is transvestite. A transvestite is, if we are going to be correct and use the dictionary definition, a person seeking sexual pleasure by wearing the clothes normally worn by the opposite sex. Or, sir, he or she could be a transsexual."

The conversation was fast moving out of O'Brien's comfort zone making him feel distinctly uneasy. His face developed a deep flushed appearance that resembled an angry bull. He interjected vigorously.

"A what! Just call it a puff and have done with it."

"I disagree, Sarge," asserted Day with a feeling of newly found confidence that left him thinking that the closet door was now open a little wider. "Not everyone has to repress their feminine side, I agree with Rita."

"Shut it, Doris!" snapped O'Brien with force. Day shuddered and the metaphorical entry closed immediately.

"Now, sir," continued O'Brien trying hard to redirect the conversation back to the matter in hand. "What I suggest is that we follow up these leads by undertaking observations on the alleged early morning activities at the Manor and having a chat with the cook."

"Er," Fricker hesitated; he had been miles away. "Sorry, observations, yes, ok, excellent idea, O'Brien, I was just about to instruct you to do the same thing. You and Day take the cook and Rita, I mean WPC Cole and I will do overnight observations on the lawn at Scotswood."

It was now Rita's turn to feel faint. She was just about to suggest that she would be washing her hair every night for the foreseeable future when the inspector again interrupted her thoughts.

"Yes, we'll meet here at ten o'clock tomorrow night and er, review the results and then go our separate ways. That will be all team."

O'Brien turned to leave the office accompanied by PC Day, then stopped, as a final thought came to mind.

"In the meantime, sir," he stated, "we'll chase up the full autopsy reports, check on the funeral arrangements for Maitland and Fanshaw and find out if there are any other relations lurking in the shadows for either of the deceased."

"Good man, O'Brien, I was just about to suggest that as well."

"But, sir!"

"Yes, Cole, do you have a problem?"

"No, but my hair needs washing and my car's in for service," she bleated.

"No problems today, Rita, only solutions! You have a day to do your hair, although I must say it does look lovely as it is, and don't worry about your car, I'll drive, I'll pick you up at eight."

With that Fricker, beaming like a cat that had got the cream, leapt up out of his chair with unaccustomed athleticism and followed O'Brien and Day out of the room.

Cole was left standing in the small claustrophobic office, her face deathly pale, staring blankly into space. *A whole night with rubber lips, I'd rather eat arsenic,* she thought as she exited the room and slowly began to descend the stairs towards the outside world.

"You all right, Rita, me duck," asked Sergeant Robson as she shuffled through the custody suite.

"Um, no; do you know of any fast working local blacksmiths, Sarge?" she replied as she disappeared from view through the main station door.

He hesitated, and then called after her. "A blacksmith, Rita, why do you want one of those, I didn't know you had a horse?"

She replied over her shoulder without stopping, "I don't, but I need a chastity belt. As soon as possible."

CHAPTER 9

"Hillary darling, come quickly," called Ball as he leaned out of his office window, smiling with contented nervousness. He had just spied the fast approaching form of his beloved jogging across the lawn. *She certainly had a new-found confidence,* thought Ball, as he gazed longingly at the stick-like figure that by now was standing directly under the sill. The early morning sunlight played on her slightly greying, shoulder-length hair.

"How many times have I told you, don't call me darling in public," she snapped. She relented almost immediately having viewed the slightly hurt and perplexed look on his face.

"Save it for when I get in the office, Tiger," she called as she moved off towards the side door of the Manor.

Ball could hardly contain himself as he waited for her arrival. He was pacing up and down when Smallman, cascading perspiration from her head, legs and arms jogged into the room.

"So what's all the fuss about, Tiger?"

Ball handed her a well-thumbed copy of the previous night's *Evening Argos.* It was open at page fourteen. He waited patiently as she extracted her glasses from the back pocket of her vivid green, baggy running shorts and studied the text before her.

"So, what is the problem, Donald? The advert reads like we wanted, although, as is always the case with these small provincial rags, they had to get something wrong."

"Wrong, dear? What did they put? I didn't see any errors," bleated Ball.

"Thank God you've got me then, you fool, without my help even that inspector would have had you in chains by now. Take a look at the third line."

Ball took the paper back and once again studied the small eight by four advertisement in front of him.

"Oh my God, Hillary, I see what you mean," he said reading the text out loud. "'Looking for a place to rest in peace, then look no further than Scotswood Manor Residential Home. We know how to take care of your loved ones. Flat now available for immediate occupancy, for further details contact—' That wretched short Spaniard took us literally, what will people think?"

"Exactly what we want them to," said Smallman. "The only problem with it is that the fool put flat available, not flats. After all we have had two residents murdered to date, unless you are hiding something from me, Tiger, and we've lost another overnight?"

Donald let out a long painful sigh and gazed down at his desk; this was not how he saw things going at all. He was gearing up for retirement, he did not want all this death, the police and worse still a large influx of new residents. His heart sank at the thought of all the interviews with greedy manipulative relatives. His eyes turned back towards Smallman. She had now turned her attention to a small pile of paperwork and was busily filing it away in a large steel cabinet.

"The natives have been restless while you were out jogging, sweetkins," he ventured, trying hard not to anger her in any way.

"Natives, you mean the wrinklies?" she snapped without glancing up from the papers in front of her.

"Uh, yes, I had a deputation from the Nixdorf woman and a couple of others, Hilda and Edna from flat forty-six, you know on the second floor above the," he hesitated.

"Spit it out for goodness' sake, Donald."

"The room where Stella Maitland was murdered. Anyway they were, at least Nixdorf and Edna were, a bit vocal. They didn't like the advert, they thought it was in bad taste so soon after the murders."

Smallman stopped what she was doing and laughed as the image appeared in her mind. She could imagine the enormous bulk of Martha Nixdorf, plus two other interfering old bats squashed into Ball's small office, vigorously wagging their fingers as he cowered before them.

"Oh Donald, you really are a fool, does it matter if the old codgers are unhappy? If the murders continue it could be one of them next. With all this interest and the new higher flat rates in place we will be in Cleethorpes sooner than you think."

She leant across the desk. With the last vestiges of exercise-induced perspiration dripping from her brow onto the opened pages of his diary, she dragged him towards her and planted a wet, soggy kiss on his already puckered lips.

"Good God, what was that?!" exclaimed Ball extracting himself as quickly as he could from Smallman's embrace. He turned towards the door as the dying echoes of a large crashing sound reverberated through the room.

Instantly the door flew open and the usually calm but now obviously harassed Langton stormed into the room.

"Ah, sorry, Mr Ball, but Hillary can you come quickly? Mr Hargreave's electric buggy has collided with Martha Nixdorf's Zimmer, there's chaos in the corridor and I think when she gets up, she'll kill him."

"You see, Donald," said Hillary as she started to follow Langton into the hallway, "there is a God, these murders are like buses, you don't get one for ages and then lo and behold you get two and with a bit of luck and some encouragement from me, maybe three."

Following their eventful meeting with the inspector, O'Brien and Day spent the afternoon tying up some loose ends with regard to the two murders. Despite all the clues, it transpired that there was no DNA evidence or prints on the bronze bust of Mozart or the knife. All traces of the killer or killers had been wiped clean. Stella Maitland's final autopsy report had confirmed that she died from a severe head injury caused by a single blow to the head. She, it transpired, had given her body to science and was not going to be burnt or buried. As far as O'Brien could gather, her mortal remains, having already been released, were in transit to one of the major teaching hospitals where a gaggle of eager, spotty student doctors were waiting, scalpels at the ready.

Connie Fanshaw on the other hand was still on Dr Body's slab.

Early the following morning O'Brien and Day stood masked and gowned observing the gloved hand of Dr Body at work. The doctor had ascertained that Connie had been disembowelled. The weapon used had the same dimensions as the knife found by WPC Cole. Although whether or not that was the actual murder weapon had still to be confirmed. Dr Body was also waiting for the results of tests that would confirm if Connie had been drugged prior to death. Traces of what he believed was a powerful fast-acting sedative had been found in the remains of her stomach.

O'Brien, with his army background, had coped well with the dissection, although in fairness he thought most of the work had been done by the murderer. PC Day on the other hand had not. For the third day in succession he had fainted and had only come to after the examination was over.

Out of sympathy for his subordinate's fragile stomach, O'Brien decided to forgo lunch.

A heavy drizzle had replaced the early spring sunshine as they drove into the car park in front of Scotswood Manor. They drew up just as a paramedic was in the process of loading up his vehicle. O'Brien wound down his window.

"Problem, mate?" he asked.

"No, not really," replied the green-overalled medical professional. "A collision between a wide load and an electric buggy resulting in an incidence of fogey frenzy."

"Oh dear, fogey frenzy, nothing worse, I had an aunt who lost the plot when another old biddy stole the batteries to her hearing aid. Horrible to watch, it was. The damage she did with her walking stick! It still makes me shiver to think about it," interjected Day going quite pale as he relived the memory.

"Any injuries," enquired O'Brien ignoring his subordinate's ramblings.

"Took a while for them to be separated and a few cuts and bruises, but no lasting damage. One strange thing though; when I arrived there was a small stick-like woman standing in the corridor, just along from the altercation. She was shouting encouragement to them."

"Encouragement?" repeated Day.

"Yeah," continued the paramedic, "you know like at a boxing match, things like 'go on, Martha, kill him' and worse; 'stab the bastard with your Zimmer, Martha' I think she said. Anyway this tall guy came up who looked like a vicar and with difficulty dragged her away. But I could still hear her shouting even when she went round the corner. Very odd."

"This place seems to get stranger and stranger," muttered O'Brien. He thanked the medic and, followed by Day, strode into the reception area of the Manor.

They both waited for a while in the blue and white mosaic tiled hallway; the silence occasionally punctuated by the distant rattle of a tea trolley or a far off bout of coughing echoing around the stone-walled corridors.

"Can I help you?"

O'Brien and Day turned quickly in the direction of the voice. They were greeted by the tall gaunt figure of Donald Ball.

"Good God!" exclaimed Day who almost jumped out of his skin. "I, I thought you were a ghost."

Ball closed his office door behind him and ushered his two visitors further along the hallway.

"Sergeant O'Brien, what can I do for you, sir?" enquired Ball, ignoring the still shaking figure of PC Day.

"Well, Mr Ball, I gather you had a slight altercation with some of your residents and am I right in thinking that one of your members of staff got a little over excited? Is everything okay now?"

"How the, who told, oh never mind. Yes all is fine. No permanent damage and yes, Hillary did get a little overwrought, but it was the pressure of everything you know, the murders, all very stressful."

O'Brien stared intently at Ball. He was lying; his face was even more haggard than the last time they met. Large beads of perspiration were forming on his brow and steadily working their way down his prominent nose. *I'll let him stew*, he thought *and just when he thinks he's got away with it I'll return to the subject. Then we'll find out what exactly he has to hide.*

"I see, Mr Ball, that's alright then. PC Day and I would like to have a word with your cook if we may, perhaps you could point us to her flat?"

"Oh Margaret, um, she is in flat seventeen, down the corridor, first left and fourth, or is it fifth on the right I believe, although it is her day off and she might not be…" He trailed off. The two police officers having given short grunted responses were already disappearing around the corner.

The door to number seventeen was slightly ajar when O'Brien and Day arrived outside. A dim light shone out into the corridor. O'Brien gave a brisk knock. After a moment's polite hesitation and with no response forthcoming he entered the hall, followed closely by Day. A quick investigation of the four small rooms found the flat to be empty. The bowl of part-eaten breakfast cereal and half-drunk cup of tea on the kitchen table indicated that Margaret Bronwyn-Jones had made a hurried exit.

"Well, Day, we best have a quick look around now that we're in. Let's see what we can find out about this 'lady'," stated O'Brien as he started to browse through a small pile of open correspondence on the kitchen windowsill.

Day made his way into the bedroom and having peered into

the drawers of the bedside table he turned his attention to a small, white fitted wardrobe to the left of the bed.

"I say, Sarge! I was right, Margaret is a Martin, at least some of the time. Just look at this," he shouted as he unveiled a rail half-full of men's clothes along with an assortment of rather frumpy ladies' garments.

"Yes and that's not all, Day," said O'Brien as he entered the room. "Good God," he added, distracted from his thoughts by a selection of chain clad, studded leather outfits that Day had unearthed at the rear of the wardrobe. In addition there was a further selection of white and pink tee shirts, bedecked with a multitude of logos and slogans.

"This is a nice one, Sarge," mused Day who, forgetting where he was for a moment, was holding up a fetching little pink number and admiring himself in the mirror.

"Cut it out, Doris," bellowed O'Brien. "As I was saying, I found this by the telephone." He handed the blushing PC a small piece of paper on which was written *"Fantasy 2.30"*.

Day glanced at his watch; it was three o'clock. "We're too late to catch her there, Sarge," he said.

"Maybe, Day, but if we're quick we might find out what's going on. Where is the Fantasy Club anyway? You should know, it sounds like your sort of place."

"Oh Sarge, I don't know what you mean." Then, after a moment's hesitation he continued. "Corner of the Fairway and Priory View in Hampton I believe."

With that he followed O'Brien out of the flat, closing the door behind him.

CHAPTER 10

Fricker was in the process of tidying up the mound of paperwork on his desk when the phone rang. The loud shrill ring took him by surprise; he was deep in thought. These were, however, pleasant thoughts, focused as they had been all day on his forthcoming evening observations with WPC Cole.

"Detective Inspector Fricker speaking."

"Fricker, I want to see you in my office immediately," rasped the unmistakable voice of Chief Constable Godfrey Hogarth.

Fricker paused; a meeting with the Chief on a Friday, his golf day, it must be good news. "I'll be right there, sir," he said, replacing the receiver without waiting for a response and skipping out the door. Half an hour later Fricker pulled up in the car park at HQ and ascended the steps to the third floor, two at a time.

The Chief Constable was generally an affable man. Preferring a quiet non-confrontational life whenever possible, although with Giles Fricker as his Detective Inspector this had not always been that easy. Now in his early sixties, Hogarth's corpulent body showed the signs of too many extravagant meals and over indulgence in the finer things of life. Retirement had become his main focus; anything that caused an interruption to this tranquil state of affairs and agitated his ulcer was frowned upon.

A sharp knock on Hogarth's oak office door was answered by an even sharper "enter".

Fricker, eyes gleaming, smile beaming, strode purposefully into the spacious and well-appointed office.

"I won't beat about the bush, Fricker, what do you call this?" rasped the slightly flushed and agitated Chief Constable as he waved a well-thumbed sheave of papers at his still standing and evidently perplexed inspector.

A trick question, thought Fricker. Even Hogy Hogarth, as he was known in the force, wasn't that dim. *However*, he thought, *let's play along*.

"Last night's chip paper? Mrs Hogarth not cooking again, sir?"

A short silence ensued.

Fricker waited hopefully for a jovial answer, but soon began to consider the prospect that this might not be the case.

Observing his superior's face across the desk Fricker concluded that it looked ready to explode. Hogarth's cheeks had taken on the colour of an over-ripe cranberry and the firm realisation began to dawn on the DI that Hogy wasn't joking.

However, never one to use his intuition Fricker tried again.

"A newspaper, sir?"

"Don't even think of being smart, Fricker, it doesn't suit you, however, you are right for once. Last night's *Evening Argos* to be exact!"

Had Fricker been a little more in tune he would have realised that this was the calm before the storm.

"How do you explain this?" bellowed a now apoplectic Chief Constable. He gesticulated wildly at the full colour photograph that dominated the front page under the banner headline "Hands on policing comes to Hampton le Heath."

The colour drained from Fricker's face in an instant as he stared at the image in front of him.

"Well, Fricker, I'm waiting, what were you doing?"

"Er well, sir, it's not what it looks like," he said staring blankly at the page.

"You're telling me, Detective Inspector, that the middle-aged tart dressed in a mini skirt lying on top of you isn't a middle-aged tart and you haven't really got your head imbedded in her cleavage and… do I need to continue?"

The mist started to clear for Fricker; Pauline Petrie, the flash of light at the door, the short, ugly reporter, it all started to fit into place.

"I'm sorry, sir, but it was an accident, she knocked me over. I couldn't get out of the way, Robson saw it all I was—"

"Listen here, Fricker, I don't want any excuses, if there weren't two murders to solve I'd have you processing parking fines before you could say Gordon Bennett."

"Gordon Bennett, sir? Don't you mean Jack Robinson, I think that is—"

"Get out, Fricker! If you don't get a result soon I'll be looking for a new DI!" Having paused for breath Hogarth continued to bellow at the retreating figure, who, having taken the hint, was already halfway out the office door.

"No repeats of this behaviour! Do I make myself clear?!"

The door slammed shut and Hogarth slumped back in his chair. He let out a deep sigh. After a moment's reflection he reached into the left-hand drawer of his desk, pulled out a half-empty bottle of malt, searched for a glass and poured a large measure.

Sergeant O'Brien and PC Day drew up outside the Fantasy Club just after four. The rain clouds had made it dark amazingly early. *Just like December*, mused O'Brien. However, even in the dim light they could see that the Club was down at heel and had seen better days. The blue fluorescent sign that hung over the flaking black-painted double doors read "Fan asy C ub" and the glass in the downstairs windows, broken in several places, had been left un-repaired. "Try the door, Day," instructed O'Brien as they got out of the car.

PC Day gave a light pull on the door handle, but nothing moved.

"Here, put some beef into it, Doris," snapped O'Brien who, brushing past his colleague, gave the door a vigorous tug. The door buckled slightly, but remained securely locked. A shower of rotten wood and flaky paint from the shabby door-surround dropped down on top of the two officers.

"Doesn't look like there is anyone in, Sarge," spluttered Day as he blew out a mouthful of black wood shavings.

O'Brien looked up and down the street for any sign of life. In the gathering gloom he spotted a dim light seeping out from under the door of a small shop, just around the corner from the Club.

"Go and have a look in there, Day, and see if they saw anything or anyone," said O'Brien pointing towards the door. "I'll go and have a look around the back of the Club."

Day walked up to the shop, the blinds were down on the windows and he gave the door a push. It opened surprisingly easily and as he entered the room a bell sounded in the rear of the building. The shop area was small but crammed full of items depicting the signs of the zodiac and astrological paraphernalia of all descriptions.

He gazed in wonder at the diverse selection of objects that protruded from every nook and cranny.

"Can I help you, young man?"

The soft slightly east European voice took Day by surprise. As he swung round in the direction of the sound he was grappled to the ground by a two-foot rubber figure of Capricorn.

Franticly he struggled to extract himself from the unwanted advances of the wobbly goat. Boxes flew in all directions as the perspiring PC battled to subdue the beast until finally, with a whimpering hiss the minimised mammal folded to the floor. Slightly disorientated, Day clambered to his feet with a vaguely euphoric grin on his lips. He turned round to discover that a slim woman, about five foot four in height, with long black hair and dressed in a multicoloured flowing robe had appeared behind the shop counter.

His grin transposed into a self-conscious smirk and his face flushed with embarrassment.

"Oh, I am sorry about the mess. I'm PC Day," he spluttered as he offered her his hand.

"I am Velda, I am pleased to meet you, PC, vhat can I do for you please?" she said keeping hold of Day's hand and staring intently at his palm.

"Hello, er, Velda, I was wondering if you had seen anyone visiting the Fantasy Club this afternoon?"

"Vhat lovely lines you have, PC Day, Stefan come and look at the PC's lines." In an instant a tall, grey-ponytailed man of about sixty wearing a brown and white-striped caftan entered the shop area from the back room. He leant over Velda's shoulder and peered at PC Day's now sweaty hand.

"I see what you mean, Velda, my sweet vixen. Lovely lines, I bet he's a Sagittarius, half man," he paused, "half beast!"

"Yes my luscious, Lucifer, a real Sagittarius, jovial, open-minded vith a freedom-loving outlook. You can tell by his eyes as vell as his lovely sensitive hands."

Day blushed even more as he tried to remove his fingers from her firm grip. "I'm actually a crab, Cancer, but if you could just answer my question?"

"Oh yes, Stefan," continued Velda, "a Cancerian of course. Kind, sensitive, emotionally resourceful, a true homemaker dear. Vat is your first name please?"

"Dorian."

"Dorian," echoed Stefan and Velda at once. "Latin and Greek antecedents and Oscar Vilde, of course that's vhere his mother recognised his sensitivity, I bet he's on the cusp vith the moon rising in Uranus. Vat is your birth date, Dorian?" asked Velda.

"Oh, um, 24th June, now please did you see anything unusual at the Club this afternoon?" snapped Day who surprised even himself with his forcefulness.

"Ah snappy, a little bit of Gemini there I feel," stated Velda as she released his hand. "Um, the Club yes, there vas something."

"Yes and if you wouldn't mind telling me, what did you see?" asked Day adopting a slightly more conciliatory approach.

"Vell," continued Velda, "if I recall correctly, because Stefan and I stop for a little afternoon joint at about two o'clock on a—"

"A joint; don't you know that's illegal, madam?" interjected Day.

"Fear not, Dorian, you enjoy your English Sunday joint, yes? Vell it's very similar to that vith, how shall ve say," she hesitated, "a little more of a kick, man. You should try it, Dorian, and release the inner you."

She leant provocatively over the counter towards him, a sultry smile on her face.

Day stumbled back slightly, his flushed face moistening as again small beads of sweat began to gather on his brow.

"Oh stop playing with him, Velda, you tease," said Stefan. "We saw a woman at the Club, her name was Margaret or Butch as she's known on a Friday afternoon. She arrived about an hour or two ago, went in for a while then left in a car with a busty blonde, but apart from that all was quiet."

"Did you see what car they left in, sir?" pressed Day as he walked backwards towards the entrance.

"Oh Dorian, vat do you think ve are, as you say in England, curtain tvitchers?" interrupted Velda, "As I said, Stefan and I vere a little out of it after two o'clock so I'm sorry, but ve cannot help any more. However, vould you like me to do you a reading please? Ve could do a discount for a sensitive young man like you," she added.

Day was already halfway out of the door by the time Velda had finished talking. With a final "Er no, but thank you for your assistance," he turned, letting the door close behind him, and walked straight into Sergeant O'Brien.

O'Brien pushed the young PC away.

"You're looking a little flushed, Doris, where've you been? I've been waiting ages."

The two officers gave the closed up Fantasy Club a final check. As they returned to their vehicle Day launched into a long monologue, updating his superior on the events of the afternoon.

"I think we need to investigate the Club and cook a little further, Day, I'm sure they have a bearing on the death of those two wrinklies. We'll come back tomorrow at six in the evening, I want you to go undercover, so come appropriately dressed," said O'Brien as they drove back to the station. "Oh and don't forget I want the information I asked for on Scotswood Manor on my desk first thing in the morning," he added, "and I haven't forgotten Mr Ball either, he's got something to hide and we're going to get to the bottom of that very soon."

PC Day sighed. He'd hoped for a quiet night in with *Gardeners' World*, but it looked like he would have to settle for a delve through his wardrobe and an hour or so on his computer.

"Should we inform the inspector, Sarge?" he enquired as the car pulled through the gates and into the station yard.

"Don't you worry your pretty little head about that, Doris," sneered O'Brien "I'll be meeting DI Fricker tonight. You just make sure you've done what I asked and are back here tomorrow evening dressed like a tart."

CHAPTER 11

Following his meeting with the Chief Constable, Fricker returned to his old, mid-terraced house, situated at the end of a leafy lane on the outskirts of Hampton le Heath. He reflected on the events of the day. It hadn't been one of the best; Hogarth had a point, they weren't much closer to solving the murders, but regarding the accident with Pauline Petrie he believed he had just been unlucky. After all, how was he to know that the reporter was going to be there?

From the present, his mind wandered to the past. Over the years he'd never had much success with women. In fact, if he were honest, apart from a frantic fumble with Janice Smedhurst behind the chemistry block in year nine, he had to all intents and purposes failed to attract a single mate in his thirty-eight years of life.

However, the fault was not his, he mused. Surely it lay with the female of the species who obviously had no taste. After all, he reflected as he preened in front of his bathroom mirror, he was 'Giles Fricker'. A prime example of all that was masculine, handsome and, there was a moment's hesitation and a final tweak of his puny pectorals, before he said out loud "a Greek God!"

Yes! and now he had a chance to prove himself right. *So Rita had said she was washing her hair*, he mused. It must have only been because she was shy. Anyway she had been quite quick to respond with a "yes, sir, I'll be ready" when he had called her up at ten past seven to confirm her address. Obviously, he thought, there was no need to ask O'Brien or Day to come and collect him, a waste of police manpower and a doubling of his carbon footprint. No, he had said he would pick Rita up en route at eight. She had put forward no arguments and agreed. He smiled, content in the fact that it had to be a date by anyone's standards.

Fricker finished his ablutions, *no need for uniform*, he thought, as they would be undercover so to speak. He liberally applied a second coat of wood spruce aftershave from a bottle that had been a present from his Aunt Mabel two Christmases ago. "Wow!" he exclaimed as he once again peered into the mirror, wiped away the condensation and admired the finished article. Not even WPC Rita Cole would be able to resist this oil painting. *A top to toe Old Master*, he thought.

Turning to leave he tripped over the edge of the bathroom mat and fell headlong through the open door into a pile of damp, discarded towels.

"God, that's disgusting," he cursed, as the week-old smell of musty socks and a farmyard in winter invaded his nostrils. He stood up, and in an effort to rid his nose of the agricultural aroma, raced downstairs, opened the front door and breathed in vast quantities of fresh evening air.

He hadn't moved that quickly in years. Having taken a few seconds to catch his breath he regained some of his poise and clambered back up the stairs.

Fricker's undercover outfit consisted of a cream heavy knit cardigan, blue and white check open neck shirt, beige polyester slacks and tan open-toed sandals with grey socks. *Mother would have been proud of me*, he thought as he made his way into the bedroom having remembered the one additional item that would finish off the effect to perfection.

He delved deep into the bottom drawer of his corner cabinet, pulled out the tan brown driving gloves with white stitching that had been his father's and grandfather's before him, and drew them over his long, smooth slender fingers. He hadn't worn them very much recently, although in fairness he had been driven more often than not by O'Brien. The touch of the leather boosted his confidence and after a final spray of wood spruce, closed the bedroom door and strode down the stairs. His descent was in a slightly less frantic manner than had been the case ten minutes before and with his chest puffed out like a prize peacock he proceeded out on to Sycamore Row.

The streetlights were on and dusk was starting to settle over the town as Fricker walked the short distance to where his pride and joy was parked.

They don't make cars like this anymore, he reflected as he slid into the driver's seat, admiring as he always did the walnut trim and caressing the leather encased steering wheel with his gloved hand. His Morris 1000, or 'Colin' as Fricker, for some long forgotten reason, affectionately referred to it, had been a faithful companion for the last ten years. With only fifteen thousand miles on the clock and an immaculate shine both inside and out Colin was a fine example of his type. Fricker turned the ignition key and the engine clunked into life. With a glance in his rear view mirror he drove off in the direction of Cole's house on the east side of Hampton le Heath.

Cole had only lived at number ten Acacia Drive for four months. A two up two down starter home on a small new estate, it was her first home and her opening step on the housing ladder.

The call from DI Fricker had taken her by surprise and caused her to hop, towel-clad from her bathroom. Having put the phone down, dried off, dressed and considered the conversation, Cole was somewhat perturbed.

Yesterday she'd had no option but to eventually say yes to her superior's request. She had tried to sound a little enthusiastic when he had phoned regarding her address, after all it was work, but there was something about his tone of voice and his clumsy invitation to go for a drink when they had been outside Scotswood Manor that worried her. What if he had an ulterior motive? *No, he's a professional*, she thought, and anyway even if he had, he was barking up the wrong tree with Rita Cole!

She had just finished putting on her uniform jacket when the doorbell rang. With slight reluctance and a churned queasy feeling in the pit of her stomach she collected her handbag off the corner of the settee and opened the front door.

"Good God! Oh sorry, I mean good evening, sir," spluttered Cole as she took a step back, her senses assaulted on two fronts. Firstly, the pungent aroma of something she could not make out, decaying logs or fungus perhaps. Secondly, the eye shattering collaboration of colours that was DI Fricker's out of hours attire. Not even the *Oxford English Dictionary* could create an adequate description for the inspector's outfit. She did not, however, have long to dwell, as Fricker's response jolted her out of her musings.

"Rita, good evening, oh, you're in your uniform, I, I thought, perhaps we could fit in a drink, meal, breakfast after we've finished work?"

Cole stood open-mouthed gawping in his direction; it wasn't the shirt; that was passable. The trousers, ok on the golf course. Sandals with socks, ugh. The cardigan was bad, but no, far worse were the gloves. The hair on the back of her neck began to stand on end as she considered them. You only saw gloves like that in 1970s sitcoms, on Sunday drivers, or, oh God, she shuddered, psychopaths.

Cole's mind flew into overdrive; it couldn't be that her boss was the killer. *No, get a grip, Rita*, she inwardly chided herself. He was with her when Fanshaw was killed and in the office when the Maitland woman died. *That, however, did not prevent him from being a psycho, did it? He could have been taking a sabbatical and was now ready to resume his deadly...* Her mind rambled as horrific thought after horrific thought emerged from the recesses of her brain.

"Are you alright, Rita?" asked Fricker. "You look a little pale."

"Oh sorry, sir, I must have got up quickly, no, I'm okay."

I was right, thought Fricker, *look at the effect I have on her, putty in my hands.*

"Let's be off then, old girl," he called and turning round with a broad grin on his lips he led the way to the car.

"New car, sir," muttered Cole as she clambered into the front passenger seat. Despite its age the Morris still had the 'new car smell' and shone like it had just left the showroom.

"Oh no, Rita, I've had Colin ten years in August."

"Colin," interjected Cole, "who is Colin?"

"Why my car of course, hasn't your Smart car got a name, Rita?"

"No, sir," she quickly replied sliding sideways in her seat towards the door.

They drove the majority of the short distance to the station in silence, Cole trying hard to avert her eyes from the big-lipped, salivating, cardigan-clad man who gripped the steering wheel with his gloved hands and called his car Colin.

With the journey almost over the silence was broken.

"So how about it, Rita?"

"About what, sir?" replied Cole who was still looking distinctly pale as they pulled into the small dimly lit car park at the rear of the building.

He turned towards her, smiling broadly.

"Breakfast, after we have finished observing?"

He looks like a sink plunger, she thought as panic began to set in. Could it be that even she, Rita Cole, was lost for words with no idea how she could extricate herself from this latest request? She had played the hair wash card and was just considering faking a severe attack of appendicitis when salvation in the form of Sergeant Tony O'Brien appeared out of the gloom.

He knocked on the driver's side window.

Fricker, who had been leaning ever closer towards Cole, withdrew to his side of the vehicle. With a frown firmly in place of the smile he wound down the window.

"Good evening, sir," began O'Brien. "Taking Colin for a spin I see and oh, WPC Cole, good evening, Rita." Trying hard to conceal a smirk he continued without a pause. "What's that smell, sir, have you had your fan belt checked?"

"O'Brien," rasped Fricker, "the fan belt's fine and the aroma you are obviously referring to is wood spruce, a fine aftershave with a delicate hint of," he stopped, changed the subject abruptly and continued. "Anyway I thought we were to meet at ten?"

"Correct, sir, but as there have been further developments on the Fanshaw murder, I thought you might like to be appraised of the situation before you began your overnight activities with young WPC Cole."

Emitting an audible sigh Giles Fricker opened the driver's door and followed O'Brien up a series of small stone steps and through a blue painted door into the station.

CHAPTER 12

During the short drive from the station Fricker updated Cole with the information O'Brien had passed on to him.

"Eleven o'clock on Sunday morning at St Martins for the Fanshaw woman. Must be a big do as it's there. I gather that the dean from St Crispins is officiating," stated Fricker as he coaxed a lethargic Colin through the dark imposing gates of Scotswood Manor. The large trees that flanked the gravel drive wafted eerie shadows across the moonlit lawn while the rest of the grounds and the Manor were cocooned in total darkness. Fricker squinted through the small windscreen in an effort to keep on the main track.

"Good God! What was that?" exclaimed Fricker.

Cole let out a high-pitched shriek as a large black shadowy figure loomed in front of the vehicle. It appeared momentarily immobile in the dipped headlights and then with an almighty bound disappeared in to the gloom.

Fricker had no time to answer his own question. His instinctive, evasive pull on the steering wheel sent Colin careering off the drive and down what appeared in the dark to be a steep bumpy incline.

"Uh, uh, uh C-C-Cole," stuttered Fricker in time with the vibrations of the car. Their descent continued until a final pained "Ugh" signalled that they had come to an abrupt, crunching, stalling halt.

The ensuing silence was punctuated by a steady hiss of escaping steam from Colin's buckled radiator.

"I think it was a deer, sir," commented Cole.

She looked across at the inspector. He sat immobile, his gloved hands gripping the wheel while rivulets of sweat meandered down his wobbling cheeks.

"Uh uh," he finally replied. "Oh dear."

"Come on, sir, pull yourself together, I'll soon have us out of here," said Cole. Regaining some of her enthusiasm she clambered out of the car, torch in hand, to survey the damage.

The Morris had come to rest on a two-foot high tree stump. Its one protruding branch was neatly imbedded through the vehicle's front grill and into the radiator from where a steady stream of green fluid was seeping out onto the grass.

On further inspection with the torch, Cole ascertained that the slope up to the drive was not as bad as their descent had first indicated. She was just about to relay this information to Inspector Fricker when his voice hissed snake-like through the darkness.

"Put that light out! We're supposed to be on undercover observations; at this rate we'll have the whole house watching us."

"Sorry, sir," retorted Cole who mused on how quickly her superior had recovered and that his comments were a bit rich, as it was he who had driven down the drive with his headlights on.

"Put it into reverse, sir, and I'll give you a push," she continued. With a grating of cogs, first, third and then reverse was selected. She braced herself against the bonnet and pushed with all her might.

Fricker turned the key, Colin spluttered half into life and a jet of hot steam straightened Rita's hair in an instant.

With a noise that was reminiscent of a dying triceratops, Colin, wheels spinning like a demented gerbil on a treadmill, slowly crawled back up the slope.

Rita, lank haired and splattered with displaced mud, continued to push; with one final Amazonian effort she launched the stuttering vehicle up and over the bank and on to the drive.

"Well done, Cole, well done," applauded Fricker who, having turned off the engine, peered out into the darkness.

The night was eerily quiet with only the steady hiss of steam punctuating the silence.

"Rita, where are you, Rita?" bleated Fricker as he continued to scan the black void.

"Aggh!" his heart hit his throat as he turned towards the passenger side window and saw it.

The figure stood, motionless staring straight into the car, its brown streaked face contorted in a hideous grimace and framed by a long damp mop of wet straw.

"Ugh, is that you, Rita?" he whimpered leaning across the empty seat unsure as to whether he should lock or open the door. The apparition nodded slowly, Fricker pushed the door ajar and the sodden, mud-encrusted, uniform-clad figure sat down on the red leather seat.

"Try not to drip, Cole, I'll wipe you down if that will help?" suggested Fricker as he half-gazed, half-smirked in the direction of his WPC.

"There will be no need for that, sir," replied Cole in a firm monotone voice that left no space for any doubt. She meant what she said.

The next hour was spent in total silence as they both stared out into the black night and then the monotony of the task gave way to sleep.

Cole was abruptly woken from her slumber by what sounded like a cargo ship's horn notifying the inhabitants of a sleepy port that it was coming into harbour. Ignoring the vigorous snoring of her superior, she peered down at her watch. Picking off the covering of dry mud from its glass and with the help of the early rays of the rising sun she saw that it was fast approaching seven o'clock.

She wiped the condensation from the windscreen and gazed as best she could across the lawns and gardens towards the Manor. A light was shining from a window in the very top storey. She tried hard to focus on this, but then a movement from the patch of garden overlooked by the west wing of the house caught her eye.

A dog, which appeared to Cole to be about two foot six in height, was patrolling a small area of lawn, head down as though sniffing the ground. A woman, who looked like Mrs Langton, although at a distance Cole could not be certain, was following the dog and behind her, pulling shopping trolleys, were a number of elderly people. There were perhaps six in total, all hunched over and wrapped up in heavy coats, hats and headscarves. As soon as the dog stopped it raised its back leg and quick as a flash, the Langton lookalike swooped on the spot with a spade and began to dig, disposing of the soil and earth into the tartan shopping trolleys.

Cole watched, transfixed at the army-like precision with which the activity took place. Detective Inspector Fricker, in wide-mouthed, lip-lolling unconsciousness, continued to snore.

There was no point in disturbing the sleeping beauty, she thought. Taking care not to make too much noise she gently opened the door and gingerly stepped out onto the dew-soaked grass. The now dry mud that had encased her uniform broke off in large slabs and fell silently to the ground enabling her to move a little more freely. She quickly ran from tree to tree towards the long tall hedge that bordered the main drive. *Here*, she thought, *she would be able to get a much better view of the activities on the lawn.*

From her new vantage point Cole parted the privet branches and peered through the gap. She was now only about forty yards from the lawn, with the hedge and the main drive separating her from the working party. Cole mentally congratulated herself. Her initial identification of Langton had proved correct and she now watched as the sniffing, spraying, digging and trolley filling continued at a steady pace. As to the reason why they should be behaving in this manner, that was a different question. To Cole's logical way of thinking there seemed to be no logic to it at all. She pondered the whys and wherefores in the early morning light when, quite suddenly, the quietness was shattered by the speedy arrival of a dark blue saloon car. It brought up a huge trail of dust as it sped along the gravel drive and skidded to a halt outside the front door of the Manor. Cole's attention now focused on the new arrival and she watched as a blue denim-clad busty blonde jumped out of the car. The, as yet, unidentified woman stormed over to the main door of the house and banged vigorously on the wood. Glancing back in the direction of the lawn Cole was disappointed to see that as the dust settled, nothing remained of Langton, Otto and her working party except a few brown patches of freshly dug earth.

"Bugger," she mouthed quietly and then quickly turned her attention back to the activity at the front of the house. She was just in time to catch sight of the blonde disappearing through the now open door.

She must have driven straight past the inspector's car; *how did she never see him?* she mused. Then, casting what she realised were irrelevant thoughts aside, she crept up towards the front wall of Scotswood Manor. Cole surveyed her surroundings and decided on a course of action. After a little agile climbing up the broad stem of an ancient wisteria and now obscured by an untamed ivy bush, she found herself able to peer through a small window into the main reception area.

CHAPTER 13

"Thank you for coming so promptly and so early, Ms Petrie. Your aunt's flat has not been touched since, since the dreadful day," said Ball as he wiped a tissue across his eye. "I'm sorry, it's just that it was such a dreadful time."

"Get a grip, Donald. The police have been through your aunt's things, Ms Petrie, but apart from that I think you will find everything in order," interjected Smallman.

"Oh and there is the small matter of the outstanding rent, Ms Petrie, I've made up a bill."

Cole could only just hear the conversation from her vantage point, four foot off the ground, but had no problem seeing the look of anger on the face of Pauline Petrie.

"Look here, you ugly little hag! If you think I'm going to give you one penny, given that my aunt was hacked to pieces in your care, then you've fewer brains than your half-witted sidekick here. Now give me the key," she rasped.

"Oh, I say st…steady on, Ms Petrie," stuttered Ball before he was firmly silenced with a stare that would have turned anyone to stone.

The key to flat twenty-three was meekly handed over and in a flash of blue denim Pauline Petrie disappeared out of view.

Ball and Smallman turned to walk into the main office. In an effort to catch their mumbled conversation Cole leaned further out from the wall. There was a loud snapping sound and despite a futile attempt to keep her balance, the WPC, accompanied by a large piece of wisteria, fell to the ground.

She sat, propped up against the wall and stared blankly out into space. Looking like a cross between Worzel Gummidge and Stig of the Dump she reflected on the series of mishaps that had befallen her during the early hours of the morning. However, her musings did not last long as the window adjacent to the one through which she had been observing was vigorously pulled open. Smallman's sharp features peered out into the early morning light.

"Can you see anything, sweetkins?" bleated Ball from within the room. Smallman's head moved from side to side and her beak-like nose sniffed the air.

Cole pushed up against the wall of the house in an effort to remain out of sight and held her breath.

"No, must have been a cat, can't be too careful though. We don't want that reporter snooping around. We've too much to lose," said Smallman.

With one, final vigorous inhalation, she withdrew into the room and brought the window down with a loud thumping rattle.

Cole did not need a second invitation to escape. Without glancing back she stood up and raced for the sanctuary of the privet hedge. She was halfway along the drive when she then had to stop and take cover as a procession of three cars drove past towards the main house. However, having avoided being seen she reached Colin without further incident.

"Sir, sir," she called as she climbed into the passenger seat and shook the still slumbering inspector's arm.

"Uh, what is it, auntie, is it tea time, dear?" he mumbled.

"Sir!" repeated Cole. "Connie Fanshaw's niece is in the house and there was a light on in the attic rooms and Ball and Smallman have something to hide." With no immediate response she shook him more forcefully and Detective Inspector Fricker slowly returned to the land of the living.

Ten minutes later Cole had repeated her story.

With the general gist settled somewhere within Fricker's brain a plan of action was beginning to formulate.

Cole had been asked to notify the station about the problem with Colin's radiator and a recovery vehicle was to be despatched as soon as one became available. In the meantime Fricker had decided to talk to the vicar alone. Having taken another look at the dishevelled wreck of a WPC sitting beside him he felt that it would not be fair even to his chief suspect to subject him to such a gruesome sight.

Ball was puzzled. "What can I do for you at this early hour, Detective Inspector?" he enquired as he opened the front door and surveyed the cardigan-clad DI.

"Just a quick word if I may please, vicar," replied Fricker as they both made their way into the office.

"Your Cook, Bronwyn-Jones, she's gone missing. Have you any idea where she might be, Mr Ball?"

"I've no idea, Inspector, she went off in a rush yesterday afternoon and we haven't seen her since, it's played havoc with our catering arrangements I can tell yo—"

"I'm not interested in your domestic problems, Ball, you've got two murders on your hands plus a misplaced meal maker and despite your alleged alibis, I know you did it!" snarled Fricker who was now revelling in his early morning impression of a New York private eye.

"Did it, Inspector? Which 'it' are you referring to, might I ask?"

"Don't get smart with me, reverend. Oh and what have you done with Ms Petrie?"

"Ms Petrie," replied Ball, now even more perplexed as to how the inspector could have known of her visit.

"She is in the process of clearing her aunt's flat, Inspector, and—"

"That will be all for now, Mr Ball, I'll be in touch," said Fricker, who, delighted with the thought that Pauline was very close at hand, cut his suspect off in mid-flow and walked out of the room with what he perceived was a flourish.

He entered the reception area, head down contemplating firstly, how he could manufacture a meeting with the shapely, grieving relative and secondly, how he was going to prove the vicar's guilt.

Immersed in these thoughts he walked straight into the back of a grey-haired elderly woman. She was about five foot two in height and was standing, supported by a walking stick, at the rear of a queue of approximately six people. They were all listening intently to Hillary Smallman.

"Scotswood Manor is a wonderful peaceful haven of tranquillity where you or your relatives can spend your days in—" She was enthusing when her flow was abruptly cut short by the unplanned arrival of Detective Inspector Fricker.

His head collided with the elderly woman's back hitting her straight between the shoulder blades, sending her tumbling into the man in front. He in turn fell forward and in an instant there was a pile of writhing bodies groaning in a heap in front of the now speechless Smallman.

Fricker mouthed a short apology and immediately forgot what he had intended to do. Moving as quickly as he could he sidestepped the carnage, walked out of the Manor and made his way back to where Colin was parked.

Despite the early hour of the day it hadn't escaped even Fricker's relatively dormant brain cells that, given the recent torrid history the home had endured, it was a little odd that there were so many new clients lined up in reception.

On his arrival back at the car he passed this observation on to the wild-looking Cole who made a brief note in her pocket book.

Help from the station soon arrived and Cole and Fricker watched in silence, whilst an overall-clad mechanic prepared to tow Colin's vehicular remains back to the garage at Hampton le Heath.

CHAPTER 14

By 3.00 o'clock Cole had, after a sleep, a long soak in the bath and an hour in front of the mirror, restored her appearance to its former glory. As she walked through the main entrance at Hampton le Heath Police Station she reflected, with some relief, on the fact that she had come through a night with Inspector Fricker relatively unscathed.

The object of her reflection was also feeling reasonably refreshed. As he sat behind his desk he perused in his mind the current state of his enquiries.

What were Langton and her dog up to? Why had Maitland and Fanshaw been murdered? What had happened to the cook? Is Bronwyn-Jones a woman or a man? How could he prove that the vicar was responsible? What were all the people doing at the Manor earlier in the day? How could he get Rita Cole to go on a date?

So many questions, very few answers and if the Chief Constable had his way, the time Fricker had to solve these crimes was fast running out.

He was sitting, head buried in his hands when there was a tentative knock on the door. He heard it swing open. Fricker sighed, slightly irritated by the interruption, and glanced up from his desk. His naturally bulgy eyes almost exited their sockets as he stared at the vision before him. A tall willowy brunette dressed in a long flowing red dress stood by the door. Fricker gazed longingly towards her and she winked seductively in his direction.

"H, h, hello, I'm Detective Inspector Giles Fricker, can I help you?" he stammered.

"Hello, sir," she replied in a surprisingly husky voice.

But, before she could continue, Sergeant Tony O'Brien strode into the room.

"What do you think of that then, sir?" boomed O'Brien as he gave the red dressed beauty a hearty slap on her back that made her buckle at the knees.

"Steady on, Sergeant," gasped Fricker. "That's no way to treat a lady," to which a smiling O'Brien retorted. "That ain't no lady, sir, that's PC Day!"

"Good God!" gasped a dropped jawed Fricker, his gaze of longing changing quickly to one of disbelief.

"I don't believe it, O'Brien, she, he looks real almost real."

"It's my undercover outfit for the Fantasy Club," said Day. "Do you think I'll get away with it, sir?"

Fricker continued to stare dumbstruck at the curvaceous constable who was now enjoying his role. He leant provocatively against the filing cabinet, caressed his red painted lips with his tongue and ran his hand through his long brown wig.

"Come on, Doris, let's get you out of here, I don't want you giving the boss a heart attack!" said O'Brien as he ushered Day towards the door, then added "I'll keep you posted regarding the operation at the Club, sir."

As they left, the red-dressed siren gave a final waggle of his hips and a bemused Inspector Fricker once again stared down at his desk and re-buried his head in his hands.

CHAPTER 15

The following morning found Fricker seated on the left side, rear end pew in the nave of St Martins in Hampton le Heath. He had arrived, courtesy of a brand new police pool vehicle, thirty minutes early for the service so that he could get a good look at all the mourners. With the exception of a balding, be-spectacled verger in his mid to late sixties, who had handed Fricker a plain, rather perfunctory order of service, he was alone. *The verger*, thought Fricker, *reminded him of a rather sad bloodhound, who, now past his sell by date, wandered aimlessly about his duties with the air of one who knew that the end was almost nigh.*

Excluding the soft padding footsteps of the canine clergyman the church was almost eerily quiet. Fricker took advantage of the silence to once again contemplate the current state of affairs regarding the two murders and associated happenings.

He hadn't heard any news from O'Brien regarding the undercover operation at the Fantasy Club and therefore took the view that no news was good news.

It was, however, while his mind was worryingly wandering back to the previous evening's encounter with the 'vivacious' PC Day that his meditations were shattered by a cacophony of sound. Fricker covered his ears as the bells of St Martins launched into a mournful toll. Painful memories of his adolescence immediately flooded into his head. His subordinate's red dress dissolved into the large floral patterns of Mrs Yates's voluminous frock as from its recesses Fricker's tortured mind recalled the image he had tried for

86

years to subdue. An image that had been viewed through the half-open door to the bell loft and had haunted him since childhood.

Each rhythmic clang vividly brought back the picture of his father, head campanologist, and pillar of village society, enveloped in the monstrous thighs of Mrs Yates as they both rose and fell, convulsed in metonymic passion, in time with the pealing bells.

The more the bells rang the worse it got and Fricker, oblivious to the small group of black-clad people who now populated the pews directly in front of him, actively contemplated leaving the church and ringing Dr Schruff.

Decision made he stood up, turned and fled head down towards the large oak doors. He crashed into the first two pallbearers as they entered the church.

Like two rows of dominos, the front cascaded into the rear, arms became unlinked and Connie Fanshaw's coffin hovered almost ethereally in mid-air, before falling to earth with a sickening thud and the sound of splintering wood.

With bells now quiet an unnatural silence enveloped the scene as Fricker, having come to rest straddling the battered coffin, stared down at the face of the deceased. She in turn stared back through a large split in the coffin lid. She wore the same look of slight surprise as she had worn when discovered hanging from the pear tree.

Tentatively, Fricker raised his head and surveyed the semicircle of faces that glared down in stunned disbelief at the scene of destruction before them.

Donald Ball, the Smallman woman, Pauline Petrie, the sallow features of the Dean of St Crispins and oh God, thought Fricker, *the short, ugly photographer from the* Argos.

"I'm doomed," he muttered and then, in a moment of what he perceived must be genius, the route of salvation flashed into his mind.

"Stop that man, police stop!" Fricker cried as he scrambled to his feet. Without hesitation he charged through the ring of astonished onlookers and disappeared behind a sea of grey slate headstones.

"What the hell was all that about?" snapped Pauline Petrie her face like fury. She returned the dean's admonishing glare and surveyed the churchyard for a glimpse of Fricker.

"I didn't see anyone running away, did you, sweetkins?" whined Ball as he bent down to try and help reconstruct the coffin. In the meantime the small reporter from the *Argos* delved in her deep, heavy bag and extracted a role of duct tape.

"I hopa that this will be of useful to hida the face," she said as she handed it to the undertaker, who then proceeded to cover the smashed lid and strap it to the sides as best he could.

After a short while Connie Fanshaw was lifted back onto the shoulders of the pallbearers and the small procession continued its way through the ornate Norman portal and down the central aisle of the nave.

From his vantage point behind a headstone dedicated to one Thomas Langton, Fricker yet again found himself contemplating a series of strange, stressful events. Life gave the appearance that, to him at least, however hard he tried, something always seemed to go wrong and it appeared that his adult years were dogged by the behaviour of his father and the monstrous Mrs Yates.

For some considerable time Fricker sat on the damp grass half-heartedly perusing the faded carved stonework. Then, all of a sudden he was jolted out of his melancholy musings by the writing before him.

Thomas Langton
Squire's Groom
1824 – 1861
Underneath this sacred sod
Lies Thomas Langton
At peace with God
His search for gold within the Hall
Resulted in his sad downfall

Well I never; could there be a connection, he thought as he carefully copied the text into his standard issue police notebook, *between the strange behaviour of the domestic woman at Scotswood Manor and this long dead groom? The coincidence*, conjectured Fricker, *was too much of a coincidence to be ignored.*

There was, however, little time to consider the matter any further. The first mourners had begun to vacate the church and congregate around the lych gate at the road end of the short gravel path.

Summoning all his courage Fricker stood up, brushed the grass off his blue uniform and made his way through the graveyard to join the small throng of people.

"I'm very sorry Ms Petrie, I, I just could not let him get away," lied Fricker as he stood face to face with Connie Fanshaw's niece, who along with a stern-looking dean was leading the funeral procession as they followed the battered coffin out of the church.

"I understand, Inspector," she said, smiling sweetly while dabbing a dry handkerchief to her eyes. "Let me buy you dinner, Inspector Fricker. Tomorrow, eight o'clock at the Pagoda Dragon," she continued, bending down to whisper in his ear. Then with a swivel of her black-clad hips, she passed by and climbed into the first funeral car after the hearse.

Fricker stood, staring after her, transfixed. Feeling both relieved and bewildered as the remaining close mourners walked past.

Ball glanced nervously in the DI's direction while Smallman whispered something in his ear. To Fricker it sounded like "incompetent fool" *but may*, he thought rather naively, *have been "the inspector's cool."*

It was while he was contemplating this overheard remark that he felt a strong tug on the back of his jacket. Quickly turning round he saw nothing. He turned back towards the road and instantly felt another vigorous tug. Yet again he spun round. This time, glancing down, he found himself glaring at the source of the irritating interruption.

"What the hell do you want?" he barked and then immediately adjusted his tone as he realised he was looking at the smiling face of Jessica Garcia Aldoraz Dominguez.

"Miss Dominguez, how nice to see you," he said through gritted teeth, noticing the large camera that she held firmly in her hand.

"Defective Insector Fricker, I take your picture again, yes? You tell me all about the man you chase and I write another story see, like the last one, yes?"

"I don't think so, Miss Dominguez," snapped the tired and exasperated Fricker. He turned quickly on his heels and marched off towards his car.

Pausing for a minute or so to gather her belongings she then followed.

"Wait please, Insector, this bag is so heavy, it is a heavy bag," she cried as she wobbled uncertainly through the lych gate in pursuit of her quarry.

She was, however, too late. As she stumbled out of the church path on to the edge of the lane she overbalanced under the weight of her camera bag and fell forward into the path of Fricker's speeding Fiesta.

"Oh my God!" he cried as, after an initial thump, he opened his eyes. Looking through the windscreen he saw the horrified face of the reporter from the *Argos* staring up at him as she clung precariously to the sloping bonnet.

Fricker slammed on the brakes and the car slewed to an abrupt halt at right angles across the narrow lane. Jessica Garcia Aldoraz Dominguez's grip on the shiny metalwork gave way. Her finger nails clawed deep grooves in the pristine paintwork and she was jettisoned at speed into the low-lying yew hedge that separated the churchyard from the road.

Fricker peered through his side window scanning the hedge for signs of life. *It couldn't get much worse*, he thought as he slammed the car into reverse and prepared to pull away.

It was her head he saw first, the dishevelled hair, her face contorted with Spanish fury as she tried to scrabble out of the hedge. With a final effort her short dumpy body appeared like a cork from a bottle.

With a screech of wheels and crashing of gears Fricker swerved to avoid the diminutive camera-wielding reporter. A flash of light temporarily obscured his rear vision and with the sound of a hundred Spanish expletives echoing in his ears he drove off towards Hampton le Heath.

CHAPTER 16

Seventeen hours before Fricker's altercation outside St Martins, Sergeant O'Brien parked his unmarked police car in a dimly lit alleyway at the rear of the Fantasy Club.

"Okay, Day, you know what to do, don't you?" he asked as he glanced in the direction of the curvaceous creature that sat beside him.

"Yes, Sarge, find out as much as I can about the activities in the Club and try and establish the whereabouts of Bronwyn-Jones."

"That's right, lad, and don't forget you are wired with a microphone so I can listen to everything you say. Any problems and I will be straight in there so don't worry."

"Thanks, Sarge, I'll be fine," replied Day as he nervously checked the position of the small mic attached to the top of his paper-padded bra.

"Right then, off you go, dear," said O'Brien who found it hard not to contain a smirk as he playfully patted Day's red-clad posterior while he manoeuvred his long dress out of the car door.

He then watched and continued to smirk as the young PC battled against his stilettos' desire to cave in at right angles and send him flying into the gutter. Day tottered from side to side along the uneven, litter-strewn pavement until, with an exaggerated swivel of his hips and a backwards look towards the car he disappeared around the corner.

In contrast to his previous visit to the Fantasy Club, Day observed that the black doors were open; the smell of stale beer pervaded the air and the muffled sound of conversation drifted out on to the street from the dimly lit interior of the building.

A bald-headed, thickset gorilla in an undersized dinner jacket stood by the door. He eyed the approaching figure of Day up and down suspiciously.

"Who are you? I ain't seen you about 'ere before. What you want?" growled the gorilla.

A little lacking in customer service, thought Day as he wobbled effeminately up to the door and flashed his red lips at the doorman in their most convincing smile.

"Hi darling, I'm Doris, you open yet? I want to take advantage of your happy hour, baby," said Day in the most feminine voice he could muster.

A long silence ensued as the doorman, with furrowed brow, continued to glare.

Fifty yards away, O'Brien was busy mopping up his coffee. He had choked, while listening to the opening exchanges through his headphones and as a result it had sprayed all over his lap.

"You going to let me in, sweetie, or I'll catch my death out here," continued Day who by now was getting into character.

"All right, it's five quid to get in, but I've got my eye on you!" snarled the gorilla.

"I hope so, dear," quipped Day as he handed over the note, brushed past the doorman through the flaky painted doors, wobbled down a small series of steps and entered the club.

Day peered through the smoky haze while his eyes became accustomed to the gloom. There were half a dozen men and women seated at small wooden tables and a further couple of women engrossed in deep conversation as they leant against the small bar. Day scrutinised the more casual attire of the ladies in the room and decided he might be a little overdressed in his long red frock. However, he put this thought to the back of his mind and wobbled up to the bar to order a drink.

"Excuse me, girls," said Day squeezing past the leather-clad, bar propping beauties. He then looked around, scanning the area behind the counter for signs of life.

"Can I help you, madam?" boomed a deep disembodied masculine voice.

An immediate silence enveloped the Club and all eyes appeared to focus on Day.

He swivelled in the general direction of the voice and was taken aback at the sheer size of the man who now stood behind the bar. He was at least six foot eight inches tall, as broad as a sumo wrestler and had a face with more scars than the surface of the moon.

Day gulped back a feeling of nausea as he stared at the figure before him.

"I'll, er, have a gin and tonic please, sir," he stammered then fumbled in his small red bag for some change.

For the next fifteen minutes O'Brien strained his ears to catch any snippets of conversation over the general noise of the Club and random interference. From what he could make out, after the initial nervous beginnings, Day was settling into his role. Having struck up a slightly overfamiliar conversation with the man behind the bar he was in the process of organising a thigh slapping competition with a couple of lederhosen-clad Bavarian plumbers.

O'Brien relaxed, content in the thought that all was going well.

Then disaster struck.

There was a loud knock on the passenger side window. This took O'Brien completely by surprise, once again causing him to spill his coffee, this time with catastrophic effects. There was a loud hissing sound from the now soggy radio receiver and the last words O'Brien heard through his earphones were a high pitched "ooh" from Day and "SIT auf meinen Knien, Pretty Boy," from his new Germanic acquaintances.

O'Brien turned quickly, glaring in the direction of the window. He wiped the condensation away, peered out and looked straight into the eyes of a bespectacled jobsworth dressed in the uniform of a traffic warden.

"What the!" began O'Brien whose expletive was cut short by the sober measured tones of the elderly council employee.

"Excuse me, my good man, there is no need for such language now, is there? Your vehicle, sir, is parked contrary to the Traffic Management Act 2004, subsection 3 of section 95A or was it 95B? Oh dear, dear, it was definitely a subsection and, my dear boy, to sum it up you are illegally parked and I will have to impound your vehicle."

"Look, mate!" snapped O'Brien "I'm a police sergeant on undercover operations so if you don't mind just leave me alone and let me get on with my work."

"I'm afraid, sir," retorted the stocky sexagenarian, "whatever you allege you are doing is irrelevant, you have contravened the Traffic Management Act and as you refuse to cooperate I will have to call upon backup."

O'Brien glared at the warden who now, brandishing his radio to his ear, was summoning the cavalry. The warden waved his hand in admonishment every time the exasperated officer made any attempt to interrupt. Resigned to his fate O'Brien spent the next ten minutes endeavouring to restore a connection with PC Day. He poured the excess coffee out of the receiver and using the car's fan made a vain attempt to dry out his worryingly silent piece of technology.

There was no use attempting to go inside the Fantasy Club, he thought, as that would blow Day's cover and cause all sorts of problems for them both. O'Brien considered a plan B. After some thought he resolved to return to the station, arrange back up and raid the club on the pretext of a drug bust. This plan, he believed, would give Day enough time to find out what had happened to Bronwyn-Jones.

His musings were cut short by the arrival of a further two wardens. A large tow truck, which struggled to reverse towards the sergeant's car along the narrow, dimly lit side street, accompanied them.

Fifteen minutes later, having recorded the names and numbers of the over-officious wardens in his notebook, O'Brien watched his car disappear around the corner on the back of the wagon and walked off in search of a taxi.

Meanwhile in the dark, dimly lit interior of the Fantasy Club Day was nursing two very sore thighs after his victory over the plumbers. He was oblivious to the trials and tribulations encountered by his superior. Instead he was enjoying an ever improving, gin and tonic fuelled, conversation with the man-mountain behind the bar. Despite the barman's ravaged facial features and brusque manner, they had discovered that they did in fact have something in common. Day was amazed when, having made a rather tongue in cheek comment in praise of the Club's décor, Roscoe, the barman, had instigated a deep conversation on the merits of William Morris versus Candace Wheeler. Candace Wheeler, Day remembered after a short struggle with his befuddled brain cells, was America's first important woman textile and interior designer. After this ice breaking moment, conversation flowed to such an extent that Day, enjoying his newfound sense of freedom, had difficulty recalling the real reason why he was sitting in a seedy club dressed in a red frock.

His contentment was, however, quickly shattered when just as there was a lull in both the conversation and the general background noise of the Club, a high-pitched electrical feedback sound emanated from Day's left breast. Without thinking the flustered PC delved into his paper filled bra in an effort to subdue the ear-splitting screech. After a short time fumbling about he succeeded in disconnecting one of the wires connected to the microphone. Leaning back on his bar stool he breathed a sigh of relief. Almost at once he became aware that every eye in the Club was staring at his hand and the large bundle of newsprint he held within it.

"It's one of those new fangled self inflating bras," muttered Day and in an attempt to conceal his unease he waved the piece of paper around and stated "I, uh, wondered where that got to, it's an article on Dahlias from last week's *Observer.*"

The silence seemed to go on forever and Roscoe, his furrowed brow now adding to his sea of scars, glared like a perplexed goat across the bar.

Then in an instant his face transformed into an all-encompassing grin and after a short pause he let out a deep belly laugh and boomed.

"That's alright then, Doris, want another G & T, dear?"

PC Day felt a gallon of stress-induced perspiration drip from his armpits while, with almost tangible relief, the patrons of the Fantasy Club returned to their previous chatter.

For the next half an hour or so a relaxed PC Day continued to make inebriated small talk with Roscoe and anyone who happened to come within slurring distance of his bar stool.

He had, however, enough control of his faculties to drop in the occasional question as to whether Roscoe was familiar with Margaret Bronwyn-Jones or Martin as she/he was also known. These semi-persistent enquiries were met with furrowed brows, negative answers and, had Day been even half alert he would have observed, a slight air of suspicion.

It was while Day was yet again clumsily attempting to extract some information, this time from a blonde transsexual with a stubble-encrusted jaw, that two figures entered the Club. They slowly made their way through the haze of tobacco towards the bar.

"Vell, Stefan, my darling, vat vill be your poison tonight?" asked the female of the couple in a sultry eastern European accent.

"The usual, Velda, my little kitten," came the reply.

Velda sidled up to the bar and gracefully mounted the stool next to the red-frocked policeman.

The hairs on the back of Day's neck went cold. Having half-heard the question and answer he now realised that the voices were worryingly familiar. He sat immobile, frozen to his stool, desperately hoping that she would go away and, more importantly, not notice he was there.

"I'll have a Bloody Mary, heavy on the Vorcestershire sauce vith a splash of horseradish and a bottle of Aldaris, thanks, Roscoe."

"So, Roscoe darling, vat's new?" she continued, at the same time as the barman lumbered back and forth behind the bar in a vain attempt to find both the horseradish and his last bottle of Latvian beer.

"Not a lot, Velda, pretty quiet for a Saturday." He hesitated then continued.

"Perhaps you can help Doris here," pointing at Day whose face was now as red as his dress. "She wants to know if someone named," he paused.

"Ah, that's it; if Margaret Bronwyn-Jones or Martin has been in here recently. Isn't that right, Doris, asks a lot of questions, does Doris. Don't you?"

"That's funny, ve had someone in the shop asking the same question yesterday, didn't ve, Stefan? He was a—" but before Velda could finish Day span round on his stool and interrupted.

"He was a Cancerian!"

"Ah yes, so he vas, a Cancerian of course, kind, sensitive, emotionally resourceful, a true homemaker, I remember, you know vat it's like, Roscoe dear, ven you've had a smoke, things get a little hazy."

Day breathed an almost audible sigh of relief and was beginning to plan his exit when Velda added, "Ah I remember also now."

"What?" enquired the barman who was staring intently at Velda. She paused, wafting her cigarette around to make smoke rings in time to the background music. "What did you remember?"

Velda paused again, a little uneasy with Roscoe's questioning manner, then continued.

"I remember… He vasn't a tart ven he came in the shop… he vas a policeman, vasn't he, Stefan?"

Stefan grunted in agreement and for the second time that evening the Club descended into silence.

Day was on all fours, shoes in hand, and halfway across the dance floor when he felt a vice-like grip on the hem of his dress. Turning to look, he just had time to glimpse the scarred features of Roscoe glaring down at him when his head exploded in a sea of multicoloured caftans, leather breeches, disembodied heads and pain. Followed by total blackness.

Just under an hour later O'Brien, having eventually woken a very angry Chief Constable from his slumbers, had persuaded him to release a van full of men for the raid.

Permission obtained they raced through the town at speed. On arrival and after a short verbal confrontation with the bald-headed thug on the door, O'Brien brushed him to one side and led his team like a herd of elephants down the stairs and into the bowels of the Fantasy Club.

The few patrons who were left in the Club glanced un-fazed at the seven large policemen who poured in and marched up to the bar.

"What can I get you, gents?" enquired the oversized barman with what O'Brien perceived to be a sly smirk.

O'Brien surveyed the room. At first glance there was no sign of PC Day. He did, however, observe a shapely woman with long black hair and her ponytailed companion. Both dressed in brightly coloured Middle Eastern gowns. They were whispering furtively to each other at a corner table and he made a mental note to question the pair at length after the search.

"We have a warrant to search these premises so nobody leave, I will want to speak to each of you in turn."

"You looking for anything in particular, Officer?" enquired a still smirking Roscoe. O'Brien, ignoring the question, watched as his men set about securing the building and delved into every cupboard, room and alcove.

It was three hours later when O'Brien's team had finished searching. His mood was not, however, lightened, as despite his instruction for everyone to remain where they were, with the exception of Roscoe, Velda, Stefan and the balding bouncer, whose name it transpired was Julian, the Club was empty. The remaining clientele having somehow faded away while his men were otherwise engaged.

O'Brien glared at the four suspects who leant nonchalantly against the bar looking as though butter would not melt in their mouths.

"What happened to the tart in the red dress?"

"What tart? We run a respectable establishment here, sir. No tarts, only those with, how can I put it?" Roscoe paused for effect. "Them what have class."

Velda sniggered vigorously, almost choking on the last remnants of her Bloody Mary. She then jumped out of her skin as O'Brien hammered his fist down on the bar.

"Listen here, you miserable bunch of lowlifes. You are going to tell me where the tart in the red dress is. We can make this easy or we can choose the difficult more painful route, the choice is yours," rasped O'Brien his eyes scanning each of the four in turn.

Velda's snigger became more nervous. She averted her eyes to avoid the furious stare of the sergeant. Stefan, meanwhile, gazed vacantly into space while Roscoe and Julian remained impassive, seemingly unaffected by the threats from O'Brien.

"Let's start with you," bellowed O'Brien as he glared directly into Velda's face. Taking a firm grip of her arm he ushered her off to a quiet corner of the bar.

Chapter 17

Following his late morning altercation at the church, Fricker had only managed two steps inside the station when the voice of Sergeant Robson called, he perceived, from behind the custody office desk.

"The Chief Constable rang, sir, he wants to talk to you in his office. Immediately on your return."

"Bugger, doesn't he have any conception of the work I've got on?" snarled Fricker, who did an immediate about turn, stormed out of the station and got into his car.

Fricker felt an uneasy sense of déjà vu when, thirty minutes later, he found himself standing in front of Chief Constable Hogarth's newspaper-strewn desk. If anything, his superior looked even more harassed than he had earlier in the week. With this in mind Fricker decided that tact was the order of the day. *It would not*, he thought, *be a good idea to suggest that they discuss the matter over tea and biscuits or one of cook's jam doughnuts.*

"Well Fricker! What have you got to say for yourself this time?" bellowed Hogarth as he vigorously brandished the late Sunday edition of the *Argos* in one hand and a news exclusive supplement in the other.

He waved them both at the perplexed DI.

Fricker bent forward and peered at the crumpled supplement's front page and began to read the headlines.

"Chaos at church service for murder victim, *Argos* reveals exclusive images of police brutality in attempt to silence the free press."

"Well! You've excelled yourself this time. What possessed you, are you totally insane?"

Once again while Hogarth's plump face looked ready to explode, Fricker too could feel his stress levels rising. At this moment in time he longed for the sanctuary of his desk and in search of comfort, he franticly fumbled in his pocket for the severed rabbit's foot and putrefied Bockwurst sausage.

It was all a blur. *How could they have published those pictures so quickly?* thought Fricker. He had only run her over that morning.

"Well Fricker!" bellowed Hogarth. "I'm waiting for an answer."

Twenty minutes later Fricker exited the office, closed the door and leant against the wall of the corridor. He let out a gigantic sigh. Even for Detective Inspector Giles Fricker this escape from Hogarth's wrath had been more than remarkable. After his initial bout of stress and having subdued the urge to ring Dr Schruff he had, he thought, excelled himself. Without blowing his own trumpet his review of the enquiry was beautifully laid out. Hogarth had, in Fricker's mind, no option but to keep him on the case. The fact that the Chief had, as he put it "no one available to replace him and that he had also given Fricker one week to solve the two murders or he would be transferred to the furthest most remote outpost in what remains of the empire" was nothing more than light-hearted banter.

With those thoughts firmly secured in his mind and his newly restored self-belief vigorously intact Fricker left the headquarters with a swagger.

Meanwhile back in his office the Chief Constable sat slumped at his desk sobbing gently. His fingers wrapped tightly around what he half-wished was DI Fricker's neck, but was in fact a half-empty glass of malt whisky.

CHAPTER 18

On his return to the station Fricker's thoughts were still firmly focused on the many strands of the enquiry. The Chief Constable had, between tirades, updated him on the situation regarding PC Day's disappearance and it appeared to Fricker that O'Brien would soon have that resolved. There was probably a perfectly sensible explanation. Day had more than likely wandered off in his usual 'away with the fairies' way and would turn up at some point. So there was no need to waste too much time worrying about that.

With the first of his issues happily dealt with Fricker turned to the next item on his agenda.

The first page of his notebook lay open on his desk and the epitaph for the squire's groom, Thomas Langton, stared up from the creased page.

His search for gold within the Hall
Resulted in his sad downfall

Fricker's face displayed the inner workings of his small mind. His brow had more furrows than a ploughed field in winter and his lip protruded in an expression of simple confusion.

What could it all mean? he mused. *How could this have any relevance to the murders?* He had toyed with these ideas for at least thirty seconds when the arrival of WPC Cole with a much-needed cup of tea and a plate of biscuits broke his concentration.

"Rita, how good to see you and thank you very much for the tea, much-needed refreshment for the brain cells," he said. "Would you like to join me for a nibble?"

"I beg your pardon, sir, I am not that sort of girl," she snapped and with a swift U-turn prepared to exit the office.

Fricker was once more mystified by her reaction to what he perceived to be an innocent request.

"I meant a biscuit, Rita," he spluttered through a mouth half-full of tea, then gestured to her to sit down at his desk.

WPC Cole flushed. "Oh I see, sir," she stuttered.

"I obviously misconstrued your meaning, sir."

Slightly flustered, she executed a further U-turn, bumped into the desk and cascaded tea across the oak surface with the force of a tidal wave.

"Good God, Cole," snapped Fricker as he made a vain attempt to salvage his paperwork from the sudden flood of caffeine.

"Let me help, sir," said Cole.

She reached for his soggy pocket book at the same time as Fricker attempted the same manoeuvre. Their fingers touched just inches above the surface of the brown murky pond that was once the top of his oak desk.

"Rita! I thought you didn't care," gasped Fricker.

Cole's hands swiftly retreated, gripping the dripping manuscript.

Trying hard to ignore the hound dog expression of her slobbering superior she stared at the open pocket book, holding it so tightly in her hands that her veins protruded like a three-dimensional map of the tube system.

"Care, sir? Yes, I care, I love my parents, I care about the environment, small fluffy animals and the lead singer from Slip Knot," she paused, summoning her last vestige of courage. "But I don't," she paused again. A little voice inside her head advised her that brutal honesty would have a very detrimental effect on her embryonic career.

"But I don't—"

She stopped, looking down again at the pocket book as Fricker stared cow-eyed across the desk.

After what seemed an age, but in reality was another moment's hesitation, it came to her. As if by divine inspiration a momentous thought entered her mind.

"I don't believe it, sir, this epitaph."

"Uh, what, Cole, what do you mean?" blurted Fricker.

"The epitaph in your pocket book. Mrs Langton, Otto and the zombies, that's what they are looking for... the gold."

"Brilliant, Cole!" shrieked Fricker as he grasped the significance of the link. Reluctantly he subdued an urge to race around the desk and hug the clever object of his desire. "Day's report on the Fanshaw family mentioned Sir Charles Fanshaw's fortune and how he lost it," he mused

"Perhaps for some reason the old bugger buried it at Scotswood," added Cole.

"Yes, Cole, that's it. Bring Langton in for questioning, her and the vicar, who would have thought it."

Life for DI Giles Fricker was, he thought, just beginning to get a little better.

CHAPTER 19

In the meantime back at the Fantasy Club O'Brien was running out of patience. He had not slept for over thirty hours and his irritation was evident to all. His interviews with each of the four suspects who had remained in the bar had been lengthy and had produced widely differing results.

Velda, the dark haired, caftan-clad eastern European, had at first glance appeared to O'Brien to be on a different planet. He felt she was the most likely to crack.

However, after two hours of intense questioning and with the exception of the 'different planet' tag he now realised how wrong he had been.

After quickly coming to terms with her initial nervousness she had been more than willing to stare intently into his eyes, offer in a sultry manner to read his palm and if the opportunity arose, his bumps. But when questioned about the whereabouts of PC Day she knew "nerfing".

It was obvious to O'Brien that she was virtually on a permanent substance-induced high. However, despite this he was sure that she knew where Day was. With this thought in mind he had finally given up trying to extract information from her at the Club. In an attempt to apply some pressure he had her cuffed and, escorted by two burly policemen, taken on her own to Hampton le Heath.

I'll see what a few hours in a damp cell will do to her resolve, thought O'Brien as his attention turned to Roscoe, Stefan and Julian.

Stefan had collapsed in a heap at about eight in the morning and despite several sharp tugs on his ponytail he showed no signs of surfacing from his drug-fuelled slumber.

Roscoe on the other hand remained resolutely taciturn. He leant on the bar, his head supported in his hands, with a sly grin still encompassing his pot-marked face. It was obvious to O'Brien that he was not going to elicit much, if any information from this man-mountain without a struggle. He then turned his attention to Julian.

Julian, the bald-headed, thickset arthropod, sat quietly in the corner of the bar gazing aimlessly into space.

I'll try the subtle approach, thought O'Brien who, although generally blunt and to the point, felt that on this occasion an innovative approach to police work might work.

He sat down in front of him on a rickety bar stool.

"So, sir, it's been a long night for all of us and we all want to go home. Let's make it easy, you fancied Doris, didn't you? And when he," pointing at the lumbering figure of Roscoe, "took Doris away it made you quite sad, didn't it?"

Julian raised his eyebrows and glanced up at the sergeant.

"No," came the monosyllabic response.

"Don't worry, Julie, may I call you Julie? I understand, we all have little urges that we, how can I put it, like to keep hidden, don't we?"

O'Brien braced himself for a violent response to his antagonistic line of questioning and was as surprised as anyone in the room with what followed.

Julian looked up again at O'Brien. But instead of launching a tirade of four-letter abuse in the direction of the assembled constabulary, he started to sob uncontrollably.

"How did you guess? I… I did sort of find her quite attractive," began the bouncer. Then without warning his melancholic thoughts were interrupted by a vigorous outburst.

"Shut your face, you pansy," rasped Roscoe his face contorted in a mask of rage. All eyes turned towards him and with one athletic bound, scattering glasses as he went, the man-mountain leapt the bar and launched himself at the emotionally disturbed figure of Julian.

Within seconds the small room was a mass of brawling figures. Roscoe was at the centre, pulverising the prone bouncer as O'Brien and his remaining four officers attempted to disentangle the flailing limbs. In the corner, oblivious to the commotion around him, Stefan continued to snore loudly. Eventually, after a violent struggle, the two protagonists were separated, subdued and suitably restrained.

O'Brien instructed his officers to escort all three of the suspects to the station, put them in the cells to cool off and then continue the search for PC Day.

He made his way home for some much-needed sleep.

CHAPTER 20

Monday morning in Hampton le Heath was a glorious spring morning. The sun shone brightly, casting merry dancing shadows on the windows of the shops along the high street.

As Detective Inspector Fricker strode through the front door of his police station you would not have thought he had a care in the world.

"Rita loves me, I've solved the crime, soon promotion will be mine," he sang to himself in a fashion, repeating the words over and over again like a football chant, oblivious to anyone and anything around him.

"Good morning, sir, everything ok?" said Sergeant Robson from behind his desk. His salutations, however, went unanswered as Fricker continued his discordant way up the stairs to his office.

At the same time Cole had just arrived in the gravel car park at Scotswood Manor. The grounds and house were bathed in the same uplifting sunshine that had greeted Fricker on the high street, but that was as far as any similarity between his and her view of the world went.

Cole had not slept well; her mind had been saturated with thoughts, horrible thoughts. Try as she might she could not remove the image of her superior's drooling, wobbling lower lip as he stared at her, like a lovesick moose, across the desk.

What am I going to do? she thought. *A transfer or I could kill him. They were*, she believed, *the only two sensible options available to her.*

With an involuntary shiver she turned her attention to the matter in hand and gazed up at the imposing facade of the house. A couple of lights were burning in the attic rooms along with one in the main office. She rang the bell and waited.

Two minutes later she was still waiting. With her early morning irritation and lack of sleep beginning to bubble over she gave the bell a violent prod. "Christ, where are you!" she muttered then with her fist poised ready to bang on the door, it partially opened and the cadaverous cranium of Donald Ball peered out.

"Yes, can I help you?" he began. Then seeing the raised arm and blue uniform he pulled back into the hall, made a vain effort to close the door and cried out: "Help, Hillary, help! Police brutality! Just like we saw in the papers… Hillary, help."

Cole was not daft. She had already inserted her police issue size four boot between the door and frame preventing Ball from closing it and was just about to explain why she was there when Smallman appeared in the hall.

"What on earth is going on, Donald?" she snapped. "You are making enough noise to wake the dead and any more of this shouting you may even wake the residents."

"Whose foot is that, Donald?" she continued, eyeing the boot that protruded into the hall.

"It belongs to that policewoman who came here last week. She tried to attack me," he whined.

"Miss Smallman!" interjected Cole. "I did no such thing, I was just about to knock on the door when Mr Ball opened it and started shouting."

"Let her in, Donald, you fool, for goodness' sake haven't we had enough trouble for one week?" Smallman said firmly.

He released his pressure and took a step back. The door was slowly opened to allow WPC Cole to make her way past a nervous-looking Ball into the hall.

In addition to the obvious tension that remained, Cole sensed an air of unease. It was as though both the proprietors of Scotswood Manor had something to hide. She stood in the dimly lit hallway and looked them closely up and down.

Smallman faced her; she was wearing a dark brown flannel housecoat, her hair was wild and unkempt and she rocked from side to side whilst rubbing her finger along the outside of her beaked nose. *No glasses this morning*, thought Cole, *a fact that made her look slightly different, less harsh maybe a little vulnerable.*

Ball on the other hand appeared as Cole had always seen him; hunched as tall, unconfident people often are. Haggard, almost frightened as though he had the cares of the world on his shoulders.

It was Smallman who spoke first. "What can we do for you, Constable?"

"I would like to have a word with Mrs Langton if I may," replied Cole. "It may necessitate," she did like that word, "taking her down to the station for further questioning so I suggest you make alternative cleaning arrangements for the rest of the day at least."

Ball looked genuinely perplexed whilst Smallman responded immediately without, it appeared, any element of surprise.

"Oh, that will be fine. You will find her I believe in the west wing on either the ground or upper floors. Oh, and before you take her away could you ask her to inform Clive as to what she has done?" She added, "with the cleaning I mean."

Cole thanked her and was in the process of leaving the hallway when a little thought occurred to her. Something had been niggling away in the corner of her mind since she fell out of the wisteria and again earlier that morning, she had noticed the same thing.

She turned and called to them both, as they were just about to enter their office.

A look of irritation swept across Smallman's face as she stopped and looked back towards the WPC.

"Just one other question." Cole paused to look closely at the two home owners. "Why are there always lights on in the attic?"

Ball's face flushed while Smallman's finger swiftly reached up to impart a further vigorous rub on her nose.

"Oh, oh the attic," stammered Ball. "It, it…" He did not finish. Smallman silenced him with a sharp elbow to the ribs.

"We are in the process of treating, eh, wood dry worm rot," Smallman snapped. She then grabbed Ball's arm turned and led him into the office at speed.

Interesting, thought Cole as she left the hall and made her way towards the west wing.

Having unsuccessfully searched the downstairs corridors, she had just rounded a corner on the upper floor when she literally bumped into two elderly ladies; heads down they had been shuffling along engrossed in a deep debate on the merits of Schubert's unfinished symphony.

"Uh oh, I am so sorry, my dear," stated one of the two as she recovered her balance. "I'm Hilda and this is my friend Edna."

Edna peered over the rim of her thin gold spectacles and looked WPC Cole up and down.

"Perhaps you can resolve our difference of opinion, young lady," said Edna, her hawk-like eyes fixed on Cole as though she was her next piece of prey.

"I really am in a hurry, ladies, I would have loved to help, but—"

Cole's protestations were cut short by Edna's precise no nonsense tones.

"It won't take a minute, as I know I'm right, but nevertheless we had better get a second opinion. Now listen carefully, dear, the question is this. Was the unfinished symphony, which was written six years before his death in 1822, Franz Schubert's No.7 or his symphony No.8?

Despite her best intentions to hide it, a baffled look spread across Cole's face. She thought for a moment and had just begun to conceive some semblance of an answer when Edna swooped for the kill.

"I knew it Hilda, I was right! It was the 7th so just accept it and we will move on. It is obvious that the WPC does not know her Schubert from her Schumann."

"I beg your pardon," interjected Cole.

"There's no need to apologise, dear," said Edna, "and anyway I wanted to talk to a member of the constabulary, preferably a senior member, but you will have to do."

Cole sighed and Edna continued.

"Hilda and I are a little concerned. It would appear that a number of residents have gone missing and we know where they have gone."

"I see, how do you mean gone missing?" enquired Cole who thought that the easiest way to get past the pair of rambling old bats was to humour them.

"Well, dear, it is obvious, I mean they are not here anymore. First, half a dozen old dears appear in reception. They sign up to a flat as their parsimonious, narcissistic relatives stand by rubbing their hands with glee. Then they take over a flat that belonged to a long standing resident and this is the question: where have the original occupants gone?"

"Well I—" began Cole, but it was a rhetorical question.

"I'll tell you where they have gone, WPC Cole. They have been buried in the garden by that woman and her dog."

"And that's what Stella Maitland saw, and that's why she was murdered," babbled Hilda before dissolving into floods of tears.

"Get a grip, Hilda," snapped Edna who grabbed her companion by the arm and frogmarched her past the stunned constable. However, she was not quite finished and as she passed WPC Cole she gave her final pronouncement. "You mark my words dear, there's more things under that lawn than worms."

Cole gawped in bemused astonishment as the two old ladies trundled away down the corridor. They were already in deep conversation about the merits of another deceased composer by the time they disappeared out of view.

"Well, they may well have a point, it all seems to fit into place" said Cole to herself. With a now slightly more cautious frame of mind and a renewed sense of purpose, she continued in search of Langton.

Her search did not take her long. A high-pitched whine seemed to be emanating from a small room at the far end of the corridor. After taking a moment or two to tune in, an anxious realisation began to sweep over her.

An electric table saw, she was sure, could only make that distinctive noise. After all she should know; her dad had been an avid DIY enthusiast and if it was a table saw it could mean only one thing. Someone was dismembering a body. It had to be so; Edna must have been right.

Crouching down on all fours Cole made a stealthy approach along the corridor. She managed to avoid all of the hazards including two walking aids, an occasional table and the three bags of rubbish that sat just outside the door of the room.

Or were they, she inwardly considered, *body parts awaiting disposal?*

Her anxiety now reached fever pitch as the whine increased to a high-pitched drone. Cole nervously got into position to the left of the door opening.

An acidic reflux lodged in the upper level of her windpipe. *Ugh, body parts*, she thought. *She must be so sick, butchering these old dears, dismembering their frail wizened corpses and then burying them under the lawn.*

The incessant whine droned on, she crouched, her body taut with a mixture of fear and adrenalin.

Her hands reached down to her belt and withdrew the police issue baton and pepper spray.

For a second Cole hesitated, distracted slightly as she caressed the shiny black shaft of the baton. The old adage "he who hesitates is lost" flashed across her mind. *What if she chops me up? I hate it even if I break a nail.* She imagined the room; a small plain room, its magnolia walls splattered with a million pieces of blood, mucus and shredded human tissue. In the middle of that small plain room would be Langton standing aside her red-stained saw blade with a maniacal grin across her haggard features, Otto lying by her feet chewing eagerly on a juicy piece of fleshy femur.

Cole hesitated, motionless in the corridor outside the room. Again a feeling of nausea began to sweep over her while from behind the partly closed door the noise droned on, louder and louder.

Get a grip, Rita, rasped a little voice inside her head. *You are a professional; let's face it if you can spend the night in a clapped out banger with DI Fricker, dealing with a criminal, cut-throat cleaner should be easy.*

Her head cleared, the short-lived feeling of sickness abated and taking a firm grip on her weapons, Cole launched her body around the corner of the doorway and into the room.

"What the hell?" cried Langton as she turned towards the door. Startled by Cole's sudden appearance she released her grip on the still humming Hoover and stared in surprise.

Her surprise, however, was short lived. An adrenalin-fuelled Cole, oblivious to the lack of carnage, caught the disorientated domestic a well-aimed baton blow to the solar plexus. This attack was swiftly followed up with a full canister of pepper spray directly in her face.

Langton, stunned and weeping, collapsed in a heap on the perfectly clean, recently swept carpet. Otto, who had been lying obediently on the floor under the window, scurried, whimpering, tail between his legs behind the sofa.

Five minutes later an elated WPC Cole marched the still bewildered Langton out the front door of Scotswood Manor, across the gravelled car park and into her car.

Chapter 21

The interview room at Hampton le Heath was situated in the cellar. A bright single bulb shone down over the Formica table where Roscoe sat. Beside him sat his slim blonde solicitor, dressed in a trim black jacket and skirt. Opposite was O'Brien, refreshed after his night's sleep. To O'Brien's left lounged Fricker smiling and humming his victory ditty, still believing that Day had just wandered off, would be found shortly and that the interviews were a waste of his time.

"You have nothing on my client, Detective Inspector Fricker, in fact you are forcibly detaining Mr Baines against his will and thereby preventing him from earning an honest living," said the blonde in precise Queen's English. She then added "Mr Baines may well have grounds to sue you, so I respectfully suggest you let my client leave while he still feels charitable towards the constabulary."

Roscoe leant back in his chair, a broad smirk sitting happily across his ravaged features. He was content in his own mind that he would be leaving the station very shortly.

It was O'Brien who responded.

"Mr Baines, or do you prefer Roscoe?" he began, choosing to ignore the solicitor.

Without waiting for a reply he continued.

"Where did we get to? Ah yes, you stated that when PC Day, or Doris as you would have known her, went outside to powder her nose you never saw her, I mean him, again."

"Yeah, so you were listening," growled the barman.

"You're a liar, Roscoe," barked O'Brien. "I know it and you know it. Make no mistake, you Neanderthal, we're going to find out where you've put him and when we do we'll put you away and throw away the key!"

"Are you threatening my client, Sergeant?" interjected the blonde.

Roscoe continued to lean back in his chair, still smirking.

O'Brien fixed the willowy solicitor with an icy stare.

Fricker continued to hum paying no attention to the intensely dark, aggressive atmosphere that was beginning to pervade the brightly lit room.

"Right in one, sweetie, and until we find our colleague we are going to continue to pursue Mr Baines and his associates. Should that create a problem for these fine upstanding citizens then I can assure you that I couldn't care a damn."

Effectively that was the end of the interview. After a few short questions, which were all greeted with perfunctory non-committal grunts, Roscoe was escorted back to his cell.

The willowy blonde remained to sit with the next incumbent and for Sergeant O'Brien things did not improve. DI Fricker continued to show no real interest in the proceedings. Interjecting with the occasional inane, irrelevant question whilst humming incessantly as each of the accused offered no further clues as to the whereabouts of PC Day.

Velda was first in. Her behaviour remained, as it had at the Club, strange, seductive and, to O'Brien, immensely irritating. She steadfastly denied all knowledge as to the location of the "lurvely young Cancerian".

Instead she chose to carry on where she had left off in the Fantasy Club; gazing intently into O'Brien's eyes attempting, as she put it, to draw out the softness that she was sure lay dormant in his soul.

Stefan followed and appeared to be no more coherent than he had been the previous day. He stumbled into his chair, quoted a few lines of Bob Dylan, invited O'Brien and Fricker and the solicitor to "make love not war" and promptly fell asleep.

As Stefan was escorted from the room a still humming Fricker made his excuses and left to prepare for his impending and, as he saw it, more important interview with the Langton woman.

Finally Julian was brought in, the light reflecting on his swollen face.

A slight smirk played on O'Brien's lips as he inwardly observed the bouncer's fat cheeks. *They gave him,* he thought, *the appearance of a confused squirrel.*

O'Brien could see by the redness in the man's eyes that he had been crying. "You're safe here, Julian," he stated. "Roscoe is safely locked up and we know you want to tell us where PC Day is, so let's not waste any more time."

You could have cut the silence in the room with a knife. Julian stared vacantly into space.

"Come on, Julie, we know you cared about him, so help yourself and tell us where he is," continued the sergeant as he endeavoured to push home his perceived advantage.

Julian coughed and slowly responded in a cracking, croaky deep voice.

"What I said in the Club was nonsense, I was tired and I have no idea what you are on about," he paused then continued. "I know nothing about nothing and that is all I'm going to say."

After a couple more attempts by O'Brien to re-engage with the battered bouncer were met with stony silence and an impassive stare from the blonde solicitor, he gave up.

Five minutes later the interview room was almost empty. O'Brien's fist thumped down on the desk with frustration, scattering papers and cups across the floor. With no real evidence to link any of the four suspects to the disappearance of Day he felt that there was no other option but to release them. A quick call to DI Fricker's office elicited a yawn, sigh and "do what you need to do. Day will turn up and anyway I've got bigger fish to fry."

O'Brien was well used to Fricker's fluctuating moods and whims so having received his superior's approval he made an executive decision.

Sergeant Robson, as the only able-bodied man available, was metaphorically dragged screaming and kicking from behind his desk.

Now devoid of his security blanket where he had happily worked for the last four years, a pale Robson was instructed to follow Roscoe Baines wherever he went and report back on his every move.

PC Day might be a half-wit, thought O'Brien, *but he was going to find him whatever it took.*

Less than a mile away from where O'Brien stood contemplating his strategy, in a dark, dank, unheated room populated by eight-legged demons, sat a forlorn figure in a ripped and dust-covered red dress. His left eye was partly closed by a steadily developing purple bruise and his arms restrained behind his back, secured to the chair and chaffed by abrasive heavy fibre rope. To his horror, he could feel with his free fingers the rough edges of at least two broken nails. Fuelled by this discovery a solitary tear wormed its way down his dust-covered face. He tried to peer through the one remaining dirty pane of glass in the cardboard covered window and strained his ears for any signs of life. He had not seen a soul, eaten or drunk since he woke and found himself in his present predicament. His head thumped with a force that indicated a herd of rhinos must have walked across his skull.

As Day began to realise the desperateness of his situation the solitary tear became a torrent and the graveyard stillness of the room was disturbed by the steady rhythmic sound of sobbing.

CHAPTER 22

DI Fricker glanced at his watch; it was two twenty-five in the afternoon as he strode purposefully into the interview room, followed at a safe distance by WPC Cole. They both sat down and stared across the table at Langton.

With any luck we will have these murders wrapped up by tea time, home for a shower and off to meet Pauline at the Pagoda Dragon, he thought.

With a contented smile playing across his face he returned his attention to the suspect.

Langton looked as though she had been dragged through a hedge backwards; her eyes were red raw and still streaming from the effects of the pepper spray whilst her hair had the appearance of a burning bush. To Fricker she looked a lot older than her fifty-seven years; deserted by her usual calm, detached efficiency she seemed to portray an impression of sad vulnerability.

"So, Mrs Langton," began Fricker. "You killed Maitland and Fanshaw, buried their bodies in the lawn—"

"Excuse me, sir!" interjected Cole.

"What is it? You interrupted me in full flow."

"Well, sir," continued Cole. "Stella Maitland was found in her room and Connie Fanshaw was discovered hanging from a pear tree. Not under the lawn."

Fricker paused, his grey cells working overtime to digest this confusing information. Seconds passed then the light dawned and his brain began to function.

"As I was saying; you killed Maitland and Fanshaw, buried

their bodies in the lawn then used your dog, along with the vicar, to dig them up and place their rotting corpses where WPC Cole so rightly stated they were found. What have you got to say about that?"

Langton stared across the table at the two police officers. Bewildered was an understatement; the look on her face gave away the total confusion that racked her mind.

"What the hell are you on about? I did not kill the old bats, I had nothing to do with anything like that or any other missing persons. Me and Otto are completely innocent," she stated vehemently.

So much for vulnerable, thought Fricker.

"Me thinks you do protest too much," he retorted. "If you weren't burying biddies what exactly were you doing on the lawn with your mutt and those other old dears?"

"I, I was," she paused. "I want a solicitor!"

"All in good time," retorted Fricker, inwardly irritated, but resigned to compliance with correct police procedure.

"See if you can muster a legal eagle, Cole, if they're not all having a late lunch. Mrs Langton and I will continue our little chat."

Cole left the room, musing as she went over yet another reference to missing people.

"So, as I was saying, what were you, Otto and the old dears doing on the lawn in the early hours of the morning?"

Langton, red-eyed and dishevelled, stared mutely back at the inspector.

"Shall we try again?"

Meanwhile O'Brien sat at his desk, a half-drunk and now curdled coffee to his left, a red telephone to his right and a large-scale map of Hampton le Heath in front. Circled in yellow was the area covering approximately a one mile radius surrounding the Fantasy Club.

It was unlikely, hoped O'Brien, *that Day had been taken far; as the time between his own altercation with Hitler, also known as the traffic warden, and his arrival back at the Club was relatively short.*

His men had searched the Club from top to bottom and all he could do now was wait for Robson to call.

Robson was at the same moment scurrying like a mouse down the Fairway towards its junction with Priory View. He had his grey duffle coat done up to his chin and its hood pulled as far down over his eyes as he could, without completely obscuring his vision. Ahead were the figures of Roscoe Baines and Velda in animated conversation outside the dilapidated entrance to the Fantasy Club.

Robson had followed the solicitor's car until it had dropped the four suspects off in a disabled-only parking bay on the Fairway. Julian was immediately despatched to the Club whilst Stefan, who by now had progressed from the pleasurable sensations of his drug-induced stupor, was furtively looking first one way then another. Agitatedly he grabbed Velda's hand and vigorously kissed her arm in a prolonged gesture of farewell. He then stumbled around the corner, struggled for his keys in his small European man-bag, before finally opening a small shop door and disappearing inside.

Velda appeared to stare in Robson's direction forcing the portly sergeant to squeeze himself into a conveniently situated recess to avoid being seen. Several seconds passed before he peered out. Robson's heart sank; the street was completely empty apart from a discarded coke can, several sheets of newspaper and a small scrawny, moth-eaten, three-legged ginger tom. The scary cat very quickly hopped out of sight.

Robson shuddered; he did not like cats.

He waited, worried and mystified, in the centre of the deserted street looking up at the lifeless windows of the buildings around him. Where Roscoe Baines and Velda had gone, he had no idea.

Robson continued to scan the horizon while reluctantly searching his pockets for his phone. The thought of ringing Sergeant O'Brien and confessing that he had lost the suspects was Robson's worst nightmare; so he made no attempt to speed up the process.

It was as his plump fingers were attempting to master the tiny buttons on the phone's keypad that he had one final glance up the street. Gazing into the gloom his attention was caught by a small window, partly obscured by what seemed to be cardboard. The window was in the front-wall on the second floor of the same building Stefan had entered. A bright light now shone through the dirty pane and the silhouette of someone could be seen. Whether they were male or female it was difficult for Robson to ascertain, as they appeared to be wearing a long robe. However, whoever it was could be visibly seen raising their arm and bringing it down with some force onto something in the darkened room. An ear-splitting cry rent the otherwise empty streets and to Robson there was no mistaking it. He had heard it many times before when sat comfortably behind his custody office desk. There was no mistaking it he reiterated in his mind; the sound was identical to the sound of PC Dorian Day performing his rendition of 'Wimoweh' in the style of Desmond Dekker.

His skills with his mobile phone improved immeasurably. Consumed with a long latent sense of urgency his fingers flashed across the buttons.

Before the abrupt tones of Sergeant O'Brien could even formulate an answer Robson spoke.

"I've found him, I've found PC Day!"

CHAPTER 23

Back in the interview room at Hampton le Heath Fricker glanced nervously at his watch. It was now three thirty; Cole had finally arrived back with a rotund, bespectacled legal-aid solicitor of indeterminate age. He squeezed his bulbous frame into the seat adjacent to Langton then proceeded to insist on being told the whole story from the beginning.

Fricker's irritation with the pace of the interview was starting to get the better of him. He coughed loudly, inadvertently spraying the table and those opposite with a fine film of spittle from his ever-salivating lower lip.

"Um, sorry," he spluttered. "Shall we get on? Mrs Langton, you deny that you had anything to do with the deaths of Stella Maitland and Connie Fanshaw. So I ask you once again, what were you and your dog doing with a bunch of zombie-like septuagenarians on the lawn?"

"I don't know what you are talking about," she replied, her voice faltering slightly.

"Don't deny it, Langton, you were seen on at least two occasions, we have written evidence that you have been digging up the lawn and we have a statement from one Thomas Langton who says and I quote,

... search for gold within the Hall."

Having paused for effect Fricker was about to continue when Langton, her red eyes once more full of moisture, interrupted.

"How... how did you get great, great Uncle Tom to talk? You

ain't dug him up have you and..." she wiped away a deluge of tears, "and tortured him, have ye? 'Cause if you have, I'll—!"

"You will what, Mrs Langton?" interjected Fricker.

"I... I will," she began and then paused. Her face crumpled like a deflated balloon. Cradling her head in her hands, she began to sob uncontrollably.

Fricker exchanged disbelieving glances with Cole then leant back in his chair with a smug self-satisfied grin across his face. For a moment he felt a little sorry for the dim domestic, but having once again glanced across at the simpering individual, he immediately discarded any minute morsels of compassion and reverted to type.

"Come on, Langton," he rasped. "Don't waste any more of our time, confess and we can all go home!"

Cole could not resist a grin. The simplicity of the woman sitting opposite defied description; even her encyclopaedic knowledge of the *Oxford English Dictionary* failed to produce a word that would come even near to describing Langton's lack of cerebral power. Surely even she would know that you couldn't interrogate a corpse.

Langton rubbed her eyes, coughed to clear her throat and in a slightly high almost childlike voice, so different from the hard exterior she displayed at the Manor, started to speak.

The verbal floodgates opened.

"You were gentle with him, weren't you? I mean," she paused. "I mean he didn't suffer, did he?"

Fricker shook his head in response and she continued. By the time Mrs Langton had finished her story, forty minutes later, Cole was on her second pen and fourth page of notes.

Fricker turned over all that he had heard in his head and after a few moments' consideration, summarised what Langton had said.

In short, she admitted digging up the lawn in search of the fabled hidden treasure and subduing a number of the elderly residents with a neuroleptic drug. Once they were suitably compliant she used them to carry away surplus soil in their shopping trolleys. But apart from this, she insisted, she had no knowledge about the deaths of Fanshaw and Maitland.

Frustration was written all over Fricker's face; instead of solving the murders in time for dinner at the Pagoda Dragon all he had to show for his afternoon's work was a deranged domestic charged with something or other that he had no recollection of ever having studied at Bramshill.

"Cole," he snapped a little too sharply. "What shall we charge this woman with?"

Cole glanced across the table. Langton was staring randomly into space while the solicitor, peering back over the top of his spectacles, aimlessly rotated a pen in his fingers.

"Well, sir, in accordance with section 22 of the 1861 Offences Against the Person Act, I charge the accused, Mrs Olga Winifred Langton, with unlawfully applying or administering to, or cause to be taken by or attempting to apply or administer to or attempting to cause to be administered to or taken by, any person, any chloroform, laudanum, or other stupefying or overpowering drug, matter, or thing, with intent in any of such cases thereby to enable herself or any other person to commit, or with intent in any of such cases thereby to assist any other person in committing, any indictable offence."

"The indictable offence I presume," interjected Fricker, "is vandalism to the lawn or—"

Having paused briefly for breath WPC Cole ignored the interruption and continued. "I have pleasure in informing you, Mrs Langton, that once having been found guilty of such felony and being convicted thereof you shall be liable to be kept in penal servitude for life!"

The room descended into uproar. Langton began to wail uncontrollably, the solicitor blustered and spluttered words of objection and DI Fricker rose from his chair, announced that he had to leave, instructed Cole to incarcerate the villain and vacated the room as speedily as he could.

When Sergeant O'Brien reached the interview room it was empty. After a brief search he quickly located Cole in the small cramped back office that doubled as a storeroom and canteen. She was sitting in a rickety old armchair, feet up on a wobbly stool with a mug of hot tea in her hand and a slightly baffled frown on her face.

"Where's the DI?" boomed O'Brien as he barged into the room. Cole was taken so completely by surprise that she stumbled backwards off her chair, cascading a waterfall of tea over her and the mound of stationery piled either side on the floor.

"He's gone home, Sarge, to prepare for his date, I mean meeting at the Pagoda Dragon. He gave specific instructions that he should not be disturbed," she replied whilst attempting to stand and mop herself down at the same time.

"Well if that's the case we'll forget the miserable bugger and get another warrant from old Hogy."

"What do we want a warrant for, Sarge?" asked Cole.

"Keep up, Cole, didn't you know? We've found PC Day."

Cole stood, dumbstruck, her mouth wide open.

"What you waiting for, guppy?" continued O'Brien who was already halfway out the room. "We've got a shop to raid, are you coming or not?"

CHAPTER 24

At a little after seven in the evening O'Brien, Cole and two plain-clothes officers from force headquarters joined the duffle-coated Robson in his recess.

"Where is he, Robson?" asked O'Brien as he squeezed and manoeuvred himself a little deeper out of view of the surrounding buildings.

"See the window with the cardboard, over the entrance to the shop?" squeaked Robson as his portly frame was condensed even further.

O'Brien stared up at the window in question and realised that the premises that Robson referred to was the same astrology shop that Day had visited on their first trip to the Fantasy Club.

"So Velda and Stefan were involved in this," he thought out loud. "Okay listen, lads."

Rita Cole coughed loudly.

"Oh sorry, okay listen, lads and lassies, you two cover the rear of the building," O'Brien said, gesturing towards the two plain-clothes officers who, immediately obeying instructions, disappeared out of site around the corner.

"Sergeant Robson, you watch the entrance to the Fantasy Club and if anyone emerges whistle."

"Anything in particular? I can do a lovely peewit or a passable tawny owl?"

O'Brien glared as only O'Brien could.

Robson extracted himself from the recess and after immersing his head in his duffle hood, sheepishly made his way down the street to his new vantage point.

O'Brien and Cole made their way to the front of the shop.

"Right, Cole, we'll enter through the front door pretending it is a follow up visit from the interview. Once inside we'll overpower the Latvian liars or whoever is there and free Day. Simple!"

"Simple, Sarge," responded Cole with an element of doubt hovering in her mind.

As on his previous visit the blinds were down on the windows. O'Brien gave the door a push. It was locked. He and Cole scanned the doorway and quickly located a small, chipped plastic bell push. O'Brien gave it a vigorous press and in the distance a small bell sounded.

The two police officers waited in tense expectation. O'Brien gave the bell a further two firm presses; the last one resulted in a slow reduction in volume, not dissimilar to the last meows of a strangled cat.

After a further period of silence Cole heard the shuffling sounds of approaching slipper-shod feet followed by the clanking of chains and rattling of unfastening bolts.

The door was pulled partly open and the slim but tired-looking face of Velda peered out.

"Vot the hell," she gasped glaring at O'Brien and Cole. "Vot do you vant? I told you everything at the station. This is politz harassment."

Sergeant O'Brien was in no mood for small talk. With the ink still wet on his warrant he waved it in her face and grasping the door with his other hand barged his way into the shop area taking Velda with him. Cole followed on behind, closing the door as she went. The diminutive Latvian stumbled backwards taking with her a display of zodiac mugs and cosmic gemstone bracelets. She finally came to rest straddling a four-foot rocking Ram.

"You sort her, Cole," barked O'Brien whose attention was now solely fixed on a dimly lit stairwell that disappeared from the left-hand corner of the room. There was a rumble of dragging furniture or something heavy on the floor above them. In an instant O'Brien was racing up the stairs while Cole briskly handcuffed a dazed Velda.

At the top of the stairwell there were three doors. The one to the left was open and a quick glance inside revealed to O'Brien that it was empty of both furniture and people. The room to the right had no door and was virtually full to the ceiling with boxes. Some were labelled with exotic descriptions like Esoteric Astrology, Biodynamic Gardening and Asteroids & Lilith while others were partly opened, spewing such diverse contents as stuffed life-sized star sign window models and cosmic calendars.

The third was shut; but from within O'Brien could clearly hear the sound of hushed conversation and muffled groans. Bracing himself for action he breathed in deeply and aimed a vigorous kick at the handle of the door. Accompanied by the sound of splintering wood O'Brien burst into the room. As he did he almost stumbled over a wooden bentwood chair. Regaining his balance he scanned the area; Roscoe Baines stood facing the door, his face contorted in fury. Stefan was kneeling by Day's prone body holding a small bladed knife to his throat. The inert PC's face was covered in dark red weals, a jagged scar ran diagonally across his cheek and his long red frock was ripped and covered in fine grey dust.

With the exception of the occupants and the chair the room was devoid of furniture. It was lit by a single bright light bulb that hung shade-less from the centre of the ceiling and a sliver of light that shone into the room through the cardboard and grime-covered window.

O'Brien assessed his options; Roscoe had begun to edge slowly towards the door while Stefan continued to crouch motionlessly beside Day, his knife glinting menacingly in the light.

Which one to tackle first? he thought. Either way he couldn't subdue both and Day was likely to come off worst of all.

Roscoe was now little more than five feet away and O'Brien

had just decided to launch his attack at Stefan when he sensed a figure appear behind him at the top of the stairwell. For a split second he glanced back over his shoulder and was just in time to see a polished crystal ball fly past his ear.

As he turned to follow its trajectory he saw it strike Stefan just below his temple. The ponytailed, caftan-clad hippy slumped backwards. A surprised but pained expression spread across his face, the knife dropped to the floor and blackness enveloped his empty mind.

"Strike one!" yelled Cole as O'Brien smirked appreciatively. In an instant Roscoe reacted. Taking advantage of the diversion he launched himself at the momentarily distracted policeman. He hit O'Brien head down full in the pit of his stomach and both men tumbled backwards into the still celebrating form of Cole. Giving the appearance of two mating bumblebees, their twelve limbs flailing in unison, the three protagonists fell backwards down the stairs. They came to rest in a groaning heap, wedged between the door and a mound of stock boxes. Cole lay at the bottom, her head embedded in the side of a large carton containing fluffy zodiac bears.

O'Brien recovered first. He struggled out from under the temporary dazed bulk of Roscoe Baines, standing on his subordinate as he got up. Ignoring the muffled groans of Cole he pulled out his handcuffs. With two swift but rough movements he restrained the unsuspecting barman and dragged him out on to the shop floor.

With both Velda and Roscoe securely under lock and key O'Brien leapt over the still mumbling body of Cole. He stopped, bent down and removed a wad of kapok plus two bear appendages from her mouth. Free of obstructions she coughed, jettisoning a fine cloud of white dust into the air.

O'Brien quickly raced back up the stairs and entered the room. Stefan was lying unconscious, a large swelling developing nicely on the side of his face.

"PC Day," O'Brien bellowed in the young constable's ear.

Eliciting no response he grabbed him by the shoulders and shook him vigorously.

"Uh…ugh, is that you, Mummy?"

"No, Doris, it's your worst nightmare, so get up and let's get you out of here," barked O'Brien. Grabbing the PC he bundled him in the direction of the door.

Two minutes later the two plain-clothes officers had, in answer to O'Brien's urgent summons, entered the shop. They extracted Cole from her box, manhandled the still comatose Stefan downstairs and called for assistance. All three criminals sat mutely on the floor, handcuffed and, with the exception of the unconscious Stefan, glaring viciously at the officers.

PC Day had recovered sufficiently to ask for Cole's vanity mirror and as he waited for the arrival of the ambulance he gazed in shocked horror at his battered reflection.

It was while they were all gathered in the shop that O'Brien heard it. At first he thought it was a hiss of steam from the water pipes, then having strained his ears to catch the sound he realised.

It sounded like a cross between a dying dodo or Pretty Polly, but either way it was unmistakably Robson's whistle.

O'Brien raced to the door and out on to the street. He glanced both ways, but the area still appeared deserted. Looking again towards the Fantasy Club he noticed a movement. Julian, the bouncer, had appeared from the entrance of the Club and was lumbering slowly in his direction.

Where the hell was Robson? he thought, but his rhetorical question was quickly and surprisingly answered. From the shadows, with the speed of a cheetah and the grace of a warthog the portly, duffle-coated sergeant leapt on top of the unsuspecting doorman. They both crashed onto the hard cobbled surface of the street with Robson, at first, having the element of surprise, appearing to have the upper hand. However, the many years of sedentary life behind the custody office counter soon began to tell and within seconds Julian had him pinned to the floor his fist raised to deliver a decisive blow.

Luckily for Robson the blow never landed. Unseen due to the commotion, O'Brien had made his way to a position behind the two combatants. Having drawn his expandable baton he brought it down with considerable force across Julian's shoulders.

It was as though he had been poleaxed; instantaneously, without a sound, he slumped to the ground. Robson narrowly avoided being crushed by the plunging pugilist. Having rolled out of the way at the last minute he got up, gathered his wits, brushed down his coat and with a smug smile of satisfaction beaming across his face securely handcuffed the bouncer.

Five minutes later the cavalry arrived from headquarters. They were soon swarming all over the shop and Fantasy Club. Mollie, the force's black and white sniffer dog, made a beeline for Cole. Ever since being removed from the box of bears Cole had been acting rather strangely; waving her hands ethereally in the air while singing assorted songs from the musicals in the style of Edith Piaf. The wagging spaniel could not be moved from her side. She sat, her tail wagging like a motorboat propeller, staring up at the manic WPC.

It was when Cole finally pirouetted a little too vigorously and collapsed in a heap at the foot of the stairs that the cause of her behaviour was revealed. Having finally been restrained from licking the face of the prone policewoman Mollie turned her attention to the box of zodiac bears. After further investigation her handler sliced open two of the bears with the aid of a penknife and a steady stream of white powder poured out onto the wooden floor.

O'Brien congratulated his team.

Day, Cole, Julian and Stefan were all despatched to the hospital to be checked over. Robson was sent home for rest and recuperation and Velda and Roscoe Baines escorted to the cells.

O'Brien breathed out a deep sigh of relief.

Interviews, he thought, *could wait until the morning; what he needed now was a pint and some peace and quiet.*

CHAPTER 25

Oblivious to all that had gone on at the Fantasy Club, DI Fricker had spent most of the time since he left the station preparing himself for his evening with Pauline Petrie.

Having bathed and immersed himself in a liberal dose of wood spruce he dressed once again in his cream heavy knit cardigan. Fricker had decided to dispense with the blue and white check open neck shirt and beige polyester slacks from his night with Cole. Choosing instead a pair of brown jumbo corduroys and an olive-green lightweight polo necked jumper. However, in order to add some additional sartorial elegance he had decided to retain the tan open-toed sandals with grey socks.

Feeling like at least a million dollars and with all his cares banished for one night he bounded down the stairs and into the pre-booked minicab that was waiting, engine running, in the street outside.

The Pagoda Dragon was situated in a small back lane to the rear of Hampton le Heath's one and only supermarket. The exterior of what was also the town's one and only Chinese restaurant had seen better days and belied the quality of the cuisine served inside by Mr Chow and his team. The yellow neon sign flickered hesitantly, paint peeled from the window frames and, as Fricker entered, the door stuck slightly on the uneven tiles.

He introduced himself to the young oriental lady behind the counter and was then accosted by a short, slightly balding Chinese man of about seventy years of age who had obviously overheard the initial conversation.

"Ah Mr Icker?" greeted the host whom Fricker remembered slightly from his one previous visit and whom he presumed was the owner, Mr Chow.

"Table for two in the name of Petrie. Mr Icker?"

"It's Fricker!" he interjected, but to no avail.

"This way please, Mr Icker," continued Chow as he beckoned him over to a small table in the far corner of the room.

Having ordered a glass of house white, Fricker seated himself with his back to the wall and assessed his surroundings. There were ten small tables in all with seating for about thirty people. On the bar was a large fish tank containing several huge red goldfish; a modern fitment he observed in an establishment whose décor was past its best. The wallpaper, which depicted scenes similar to those shown on Wedgwood plates, showed signs of wear in numerous places and the large plaster model, which stood by the door and resembled a komodo dragon, had lost a number of its teeth and scales.

With the exception of Fricker there were only two other customers in the room. A middle-aged man with a flushed red face and immense proportions lounged back in his undersized chair surveying his Cantonese fillet steak, egg fried rice and prawn crackers. His slender young female companion nibbled tentatively on mixed vegetable chow mein and laughed nervously at his jokes.

Fricker checked his watch; *it was eight fifteen, but it was a woman's prerogative to be late*, he mused.

The sudden reappearance of Chow interrupted Fricker's thoughts.

"You have little nibble while you wait, Mr Icker?"

A disgusted look of disdain spread across Fricker's rubbery lips as he shifted uncomfortably in his chair.

"I beg your pardon, Mr Chow, I thought this was a decent establishment and anyway even if it's not... I'm not that sort of man!" snapped the agitated DI.

Chow stared back inscrutably, while in the background the middle-aged man of immense proportions spluttered and choked on a prawn cracker.

"Mr Icker, you like roast plum duck puffs why you wait for lady?"

This was the final straw for Fricker, the strain of a day's interviewing boiled over; face flushed with rage he stood up pushing his chair over in the process.

Even at five foot six on tiptoes Fricker still managed to tower over Chow who continued to stare impassively at the pontificating, posturing policeman.

"I'm not that way inclined, Mr Chink," rasped a puce Fricker who, gesticulating wildly, inadvertently raised his arm.

Instantly Chow was transformed from gentle oriental to an antique martial arts expert. Swift as a flash he adopted a crouched kung fu horse-riding stance and delivered a roundhouse kick to the side of Fricker's head.

It was as though he had been shot with a stun gun; legs buckling he collapsed in a heap across the table scattering the place settings as he landed. Chow moved in for the kill.

"Nobody calls me Mr Chink not even Mr Icker of the Yad," he calmly stated, as arm raised he prepared to deliver a final chop to the neck.

"Mr Chow! Leave Detective Inspector Fricker alone now!"

Chow turned towards the door and stared straight at Pauline Petrie. She had entered the restaurant as the two other diners scurried out of the door. The transformation was immediate, in a moment he turned from deadly assassin to submissive chef. He bowed, turned back towards the prostrate form of Fricker, lifted him up by his collar, placed him back in his chair and dusted him down.

Having re-laid the table Chow bowed once again and made his way back to the kitchen.

"Sorry about that, Giles, Mr Chow can be a little sensitive at times," said Petrie as she slipped her body into the seat opposite the woozy Fricker.

Fricker was still a little concussed. His unfocused eyes wandered aimlessly then settled on the four massive breasts that filled his field of vision.

"Thank you, Ms Petrie," he mumbled as he gazed adoringly across the table shaking his head in an attempt to restore some calm to his battered brain.

Petrie gazed back at Fricker. She was, as seemed to be her custom, dressed in a tight black lycra top, blue denim skirt, black fishnet tights and red stilettos. "So Giles, how is your head?"

Fricker gave his skull one final shake, reluctantly raised his eyes from the objects of his affection and mumbled a response.

"Oh er, I'm ok thank you, Ms Petrie. I'm not sure what happened... did you see?"

"No, Giles, I think you slipped and banged your head," she said beckoning Mr Chow with a click of her fingers. "Shall we order?"

Fricker's lower lip drooped even lower than usual as he endeavoured to remember what had happened to him two minutes before.

"Oh er... Ms Petrie, what do you recommend?"

Petrie licked her lips and leaned provocatively across the table towards the disorientated Detective Inspector.

"For you, Giles," she said softly, "Shrimps Foo Yung."

"And for, for you?" he drooled.

"Wandering dragon, beef and," she paused, "oyster sauce. Oh, and a shaojiu."

Mr Chow smirked, bowed and retreated backwards through the double doors into the kitchen.

The restaurant had suddenly become busy. Four twenty-something couples had arrived and were now sitting in the window seats to the left of Fricker's table while a group of five nuns in full habits sat directly in front. To their right with her back to Petrie sat a very small dumpy woman with long highlighted hair. In the half-light Fricker felt, just for a moment, that he recognised her.

However, as she bent down to delve into a big black bag on the floor he lost interest and turned his attention back to his companion.

Petrie continued to flaunt her assets and make small talk. Fricker tried hard to keep his brain focused on the conversation.

"Your meal, Mr Icker," interjected Chow. "Oh, and your shaojiu," he added with an inscrutable grin.

"Cheers, Giles," said Petrie as she downed her glass in one gulp.

Fricker eyed his glass and raised it to the end of his long proboscis. *It did not look like a gin and tonic*, he thought. He closed his eyes, paused and took a long swig of the warm liquid.

It was like, he imagined, drinking molten lava. A burning sensation seared its way past his epiglottis and down his throat while rivulets of perspiration snaked down his flushed cheek.

"Whow! Fire water," he wheezed.

"Mr Chow, a top up for Mr Fricker before you go."

Two hours later a replete and inebriated Fricker leant back in his chair. He felt so laid back he was almost horizontal. As he peered across the table beyond Petrie the room became a hazy blur. Any attempt to focus on his companion had to be abandoned; her face, chest and body merged and rotated like a kaleidoscope as he struggled to keep mind and eyes in unison.

"Soooo, Pauline, how about an incy wincy bit more drinky winky?"

"Oh, Giles, you are a tease, tell me a little more about how your investigation is going and I'll see what Mr Chow has in his cellar?"

"What do you want to know, Paulinniewiney?"

"Well, Giles, have you found the missing cook?"

"Oh ha, ha, you mean the culinary cross-dresser!" blurted Fricker a little too loudly. The room went quiet and the five nuns turned their heads towards his table and glared in abhorrence.

Fricker leaned across to his companion and whispered conspiratorially.

"No, Pauline, we have not found her." He chuckled then continued. "Perhaps, ha, ha, she's cooked her own goose if you know what I mean!"

She half-laughed, and then grimaced as she looked across the table at the steadily deteriorating Detective Inspector.

His protruding lower lip seemed to have taken on astronomically large proportions as he grinned and leaned forwards then backwards, leering and salivating in her direction.

"No luck with the cook then. Have you had any success in finding the murderer, Giles?"

He beckoned her to come a little closer and she reluctantly moved into his air space.

"It was the vicar," he blurted out, emitting as he did, an enormous shrimp and prawn fuelled burp. Petrie reeled backwards gasping for oxygen.

"The, the vicar. Which vicar?"

"Oh you know, the one at the Manor; tall, gangly, old bloke, I can't quite recall his name," he slurred. "Now how about Mr Chow's cellar?"

"Ball!"

"Don't be so rude, Paulini. Where's Mr Chowy and his fire water?"

"You mean it was Mr Ball?" she continued.

"Yes, yes, now let's talk about something more interesting like Mr Choy and his lovely cellar!"

Petrie smiled a contented smile, clicked her fingers and waited.

Two minutes later Chow appeared at her side. She bent over and whispered in his ear, and with a sly grin he bowed to Fricker and, miraculously avoiding the other diners, walked backwards towards the kitchen.

"More drinky winky?" enquired Fricker.

"Be patient, Giles, everything comes to those that wait."

Fricker's eyes wandered about the room. The group of young people had now left, leaving the short dumpy woman and the five nuns. The latter were quietly perusing the sweet menu; debating the contrasting merits of mango pudding and ginger ice cream. He slowly turned his attention back to his own table and finding that Chow had silently appeared at his elbow nearly jumped out of his skin. His cry of "Good God! Mr Chung!" was greeted by further glares and muttered disapproval from the nuns. An additional "What the devil is that!" further compounded the sin as Fricker stared at the glass bottle that Chow had placed in the centre of the table.

The bottle contained a small red and yellow snake, pickled in a putrid coloured liquid.

"This is snake wine, Mr Icker. Traditional Chinese restorative; we put large nasty venomous snake in jar with rice wine, add medicinal herbs and leave it to stew for many months. Only real men like you, Mr Icker, can handle it," added Chow.

Petrie downed her drink in one go, winked at Fricker and poured herself another glass.

"Your turn, big boy!"

Can't be any worse than the shaojiu, his bewildered brain observed. Once again Fricker sniffed the glass, held his breath and poured the liquid down his throat.

It was! He stood up gasping for air; his eyes watered, further obscuring his vision as his hands blindly waved from side to side franticly searching for water. Within seconds he had caused havoc. His grasping, groping hands launched the open bottle of wine into the air, jettisoning the smelly serpent across the room into the lap of the mother superior. Fricker stumbled forward across the table, landing face down, with his nose once again firmly imbedded between the twin peaks of Petrie's cleavage. The nuns screamed, Chow ran from the kitchen armed with a cleaver and the short dumpy woman foraged in her big black bag.

As Fricker slowly raised his head there was a bright flash and it came back to him; Jessica Garcia Aldoraz Dominguez was the name of the short, fat dumpy woman. That awful fact was the last thing he remembered before a right hook from Petrie sent him once again into oblivion.

CHAPTER 26

Late Tuesday morning in Detective Inspector Fricker's Hampton le Heath office was more like Accident and Emergency than a Police Station. Fricker sat slumped at his desk nursing two large throbbing black eyes. Seated opposite were PC Day and WPC Cole. Sergeant O'Brien leant against the filing cabinet. Day's face was swollen and the jagged scar on his left cheek looked raw and angry. Cole was battling the unpleasant comedown from cocaine. She felt irritable, lethargic and her head throbbed with the feet of a hundred elephants. O'Brien observed the scene with a feeling of despair. *Why*, he thought, *had he been so unfortunate as to end up working with such a bunch of dysfunctional public servants?*

Fricker's mind was a mess. He could not remember anything from the previous night except a slight recollection of a bright flashing light and the image of a hysterical nun, her black habit flapping like a demented bat as she wrestled with a decomposing snake. As to how he got home he had no idea.

"What are we doing here, Sergeant?" mumbled Fricker who, without waiting for a reply, continued. "Uh… perhaps you ought to lead this meeting, O'Brien. But don't shout."

Having spent the last three hours in the interview room O'Brien was in no mood to pander to their sensibilities.

"Right! Okay, team," boomed O'Brien. "Let's have a recap."

Fricker visibly jumped out of his skin while a whimpering Day covered his ears.

"Hey, Sarge, steady with the volume, man," drawled Cole as she lounged back in her chair.

"Right! Roscoe, Velda and his drug dealing team have finally spilled the beans. The Fantasy Club was a front for their trafficking activities and they mistook Doris here for a proper undercover drugs squad officer."

PC Day raised his eyes and painfully grinned with pride.

"You mean they thought I was a real officer?"

"Sadly yes," replied O'Brien who then added, "just shows how stupid they are, doesn't it!"

Day slumped deflated into his chair whilst Fricker disappeared under his desk.

"Get a grip, Doris, you know you make a better tart than a policeman," interjected Cole.

"Quiet children!" snapped O'Brien. "We still have two murders to solve, so let's get our act together and," he paused and then scanned the room. "Where's DI Fricker? Did anyone see him leave?"

Cole looked at Day and shrugged her shoulders.

"Hey, man," she drawled. "One minute he was sitting down in that chair like and then man... whoosh, he's gone like in a puff."

Day's eyes widened, but before he could utter a word O'Brien hammered his fist down on the desk. Two pens, a selection of paper clips and a cloud of dust flew out of an empty honey jar while the cold contents of a china cup leapt into the air scattering the brown fluid across the paper-strewn desktop. The room descended into silence and a muffled voice from the inner recesses of the footwell bleated, "Dr Schruff, is that you?"

O'Brien, Cole and Day peered over the edge of the desk and watched as a hand appeared clutching a now familiar squelchy plastic bag.

"Oh God, not that again?" mouthed Cole as she stared in horror at the severed rabbit's foot and putrefied Bockwurst sausage as they loomed into view. The dishevelled panda-eyed head of her superior closely followed.

"Uh…just looking for my pen, team," he stated before clambering back into his chair and replacing the telephone receiver.

O'Brien ignored his superior.

"Anyone got any ideas about the Fanshaw and Maitland murders?"

"Who?" enquired Cole.

Sergeant O'Brien flashed a look of pure contempt at the WPC and continued.

"The answer to these murders has to be found at the Manor. We need to find Bronwyn-Jones; when we do the whole picture will be a lot clearer. Day and Cole, I want you to go back to Scotswood and re-question Ball and Smallman. I will go back to see Dr Body. There must be some clues that he's missed. Any questions?"

Cole, Day and Fricker all put their hands up at once.

O'Brien's heart sank.

"One at a time," he said as his glance rested on the face of the DI. "Yes, sir?" O'Brien queried.

"What would you like me to do, Sergeant?" bleated Fricker, his lip pouting like a truculent schoolboy.

"The most useful thing you can do, sir," he hesitated holding back a desire to voice his frustrations, "is to man the phones and coordinate things from here."

PC Day waved his arm vigorously. "Me, Sarge, me!"

"Yes," rasped O'Brien.

"What should I ask them, Sarge?"

Ignoring what he viewed as a totally inane question O'Brien turned his focus on Cole who was gently waving her hand as though it was the sail of a ship.

"Cole, tell Day what you are going to talk to the gruesome twosome at the Manor about."

"Hey, Day, baby," she drawled. "We going to see if they topped the oldies and find out where they hid the other old dears, ain't that right, Sarge?"

O'Brien's ears pricked up after Cole's final statement.

"The other old dears, Cole? What do you mean by that?" he asked. However, before she could answer DI Fricker raised his head from his desk and interrupted.

"She's referring to something the Langton woman muttered," he paused slightly as he tried to reinvigorate his sleepy brain cells. "Something about other missing persons, I believe, Sergeant."

"Yeah, boss, that's right; Langton and the two old bats Hedna, and Eilder were their names. They said that some of the older residents were missing. Under the lawn they thought." Having controlled herself for less than thirty seconds she added, "Hey, man, they must have groovy turf sheets."

"Okay, Cole, go and get yourself sobered up. Day can drive and I want a result by tomorrow morning!" snapped O'Brien.

"Yes, Sarge!" they all replied in unison, then Day and a wobbly Cole followed by a subdued Fricker filed out through the door.

O'Brien stared out of the window in disbelief, shook his head sadly and followed them out of the office.

CHAPTER 27

At Scotswood Manor an air of relief emanated from Ball's office. He sat, feet up on his desk with a smug self-satisfied grin across his usually dour features. Smallman was relaxing opposite in a brown leather armchair that almost totally enveloped her small frame.

"Look at this one, Donald!" she said, vigorously waving the particulars of a brand new mobile home in his direction. "It's only £12,500 and on a lovely site just behind the Cleethorpes light railway."

"That sounds grand, sweetkins. Now the police have got Langton in custody they should leave us alone. Who would have thought our domestic would have been a double murderer?"

"The hacker with a hoover," replied Smallman before they dissolved in to maniacal howls of laughter at her rare venture into the world of comedy.

Their mirth was cut short by a sharp knock at the door. Without pausing for an answer Clive shuffled in and stood staring at them both. Tears were streaming down Ball's face and Smallman was slouching, helpless with laughter in her chair.

"Scuse me, sir…"

"What is it, Clive… found another body?" howled Ball.

Clive stood at the door a deadpan expression on his face.

"Uh. No, sir, there's," he hesitated.

"Get on with it, we've got some celebrating to do!" snapped Hillary who could never cope with interruptions at the best of times and to her, this was the best of times.

"There are two coppers to see you, Mr Ball, sir!"

The faces of Smallman and Ball dropped simultaneously.

"Coppers," whined Ball. "Do you mean policemen, Clive?"

Clive nodded in response and without waiting for further instructions limped out of the room.

Smallman glared across the room at Ball with a look that fluctuated between incredulousness, hatred and horror.

"What have you done, Donald? You'd better not have forgotten to pay your library fines again, you dozy fool. Leave the talking to me. Do you understand?"

Ball nodded in meek acquiescence. Aware that any argument would be a waste of time he made his way out of the office towards the front door.

Back at the police station Detective Inspector Fricker yet again sat, head in hands. His eyes throbbed. Having just begun to feel slightly human and regain a little of his cerebral functions he was contemplating life and reflecting on how poorly he had handled the recent meeting.

I'm the man in charge, he thought as he visualised his wimpish behaviour and the sheepish way he had followed Day and Cole out of the office. *I must get a grip and gird my loins or as Hogarth had said I'll be processing parking fines before I can say Gordon Bennett.*

With substantial mental effort, his loins now partially girded, Fricker stood up. He puffed out his small chest then immediately slumped back into his chair as the shrill ring of his telephone shattered the quiet of his office.

"Who the hell is that?" he moaned to himself, indignant at being interrupted at such a crucial point. "Yes!"

"Defective Chef Inspector Frickur?" asked the faintly familiar voice at the end of the line. "You do not a know me, but I know a you."

"Who is this?" Fricker interjected in an irritated manner.

"I no tell you that, but I have some think that you might, how you say… want!"

Fricker tried hard to rack his brains. The voice was tantalisingly familiar, but for the life of him he could not conjure up the name.

"Look, madam. I don't know who you are, but stop messing about. What is it you want?"

"Don't snap, Insector, or I'll again have to pass this on to your supearia. I have, how you say… an interesting picture and unless you pay me a thousand euros I shall have to get it a printed!"

A bead of sweat began to wriggle down his forehead and onto his nose and his armpits suddenly began to leak perspiration.

"Okay. Where do you want to meet?" Fricker snapped.

"That's a bit bitter, Insector. Seven tonight at the Church of the Immaculate Conception on Priory Lane, bueno?"

"Bue… what?" he asked then continued, "I'll be there" and hung up the now dead receiver.

Resuming his despondent head in hands posture he tried hard to remember the name of the woman on the phone. He glanced at his watch. It was two thirty; *only four and a half hours before he found out*, he thought. Surely he would remember by then.

At Headquarters Sergeant O'Brien was enjoying the relative peace and quiet while he waited for Dr Body to appear from his office. O'Brien was finding it more and more difficult to understand the fluctuating moods of his superior. After almost five years working together he thought he would be more in tune with the DI, but in reality he found his constant ramblings and desire to hide beneath his desk harder to cope with. *It had never been like that in the forces*, he thought.

O'Brien was still musing when Dr Body bustled out into the corridor adjusting his glasses with one hand and shaping his minimal thatch with the other.

"What can I do for you, Sergeant?" he enquired in a genial manner.

O'Brien explained in as brief a way as he could the impasse they had reached in the search for the killer, or killers, of Fanshaw and Maitland.

Dr Body scratched his ear, whistled through his teeth and glanced at his watch. *Too early even for him to be contemplating a drink*, thought O'Brien. He badgered the doctor a little further.

"Anything, Doc, anything unusual on either of the bodies that might help, however small?"

"No, Sergeant, nothing on the bodies, but," he paused. "Oh, there was…"

"There was what?" queried an eager O'Brien.

"Oh, just something I read in a medical paper recently. About people who suffer from dyscalculia."

"Dis what?" interrupted O'Brien

"It's a maths disability, people have difficulty with numbers. Having read this I was thinking about the article and thinking about the murders and I thought—"

"Yes?"

"I thought, well, as the first woman lived at twenty-three and the second at thirty-two—"

"The other way round, thirty-two then twenty-three," stated the very precise O'Brien.

"Well whichever," continued the doctor. "If the murderer has dyscalculia then perhaps he or she never meant to murder the first woman at all."

"What do you mean?"

"I mean perhaps they misread the door numbers and battered the old dear in error. Perhaps they only meant to kill the woman in number twenty-three all along."

O'Brien gasped. "Well I never, you may be on to something, Doc!"

"But then again I'd had a few scotches at the time, so who knows!"

The doctor laughed and with a parting "I hope that helps" disappeared back into his office.

O'Brien stood in the corridor, his expression fluctuating between perplexed and self-satisfied. *It might just be*, he thought, *that we are getting somewhere at last!*

At Scotswood Manor there was a subdued silence in the office. Having shown PC Day and WPC Cole into the room Ball had deposited himself back at his desk while Smallman remained seated in her cavernous armchair, glaring over the top of her glasses.

How dare they spoil what was such a happy day, she seethed inwardly.

A somewhat less spaced out Cole was leading the questioning while Day took copious notes in his neat, copperplate handwriting.

"Let's go through it again, Mr Ball. A source, which I cannot name, has intimated that some of your residents have, how shall I put it, gone missing!"

"I'm sorry, miss, I mean Constable, I don't know what you mean," replied Ball whose pause for breath was filled by an interjection from Smallman.

"Yes, we have lost two residents."

Cole raised her eyebrows and followed up with her best Gestapo interrogation impression.

"So you admit to having lost two old dears! Continue if you please, Miss Smallman."

"Maitland and Fanshaw obviously, Constable!"

PC Day's pencil was going ten to the dozen.

"Look, Miss Smallman, let's not play games, shall we? What other residents have gone away, shall we say?"

Smallman looked puzzled. She scratched her nose with a long bony finger and began to reply.

"WPC Cole, far from losing people, the fact is we have more residents now than we ever had."

Ball looked anxiously in her direction. She ignored his pleading eyes and continued.

"After—"

Her response was cut short by an ear-splitting scream that made all in the office stop and stare in the direction of the garden. The blood in their veins ran cold and goose bumps covered their skin.

"Oh my God, what was that?" echoed Cole and Day in unison.

CHAPTER 28

In their room on the second floor of the west wing Hilda and Edna looked at each other. "Without a doubt this was definitely a middle C," stated Edna with authoritative conviction.

Hilda did not even consider saying a word. She just nodded.

It was not, she thought, *even worth attempting to contradict her perverse friend and much as it pained her to do so, she decided to agree.*

Cole reached the garden first, trailed closely by Day, his rosy red-scarred cheeks glowing with the exertion. Smallman and Ball followed slowly.

After a moment's hesitation they stopped, waited and watched as the two police officers gingerly made their way across the lawn. A lone figure of average height and mountainous width stood ashen-faced in front of the old wooden slatted compost heap; her short ginger-haired head shaking in muted disbelief.

PC Day had begun to lag behind his colleague, reluctant after his recent experiences to see anything that might make him faint.

"You look first, Rita, it's probably nothing to worry about," he mumbled.

"Bloody wuss," was the acid reply as Cole walked up to the figure.

"Who are you then and what's all this noise about?" she barked.

Oblivious to Cole's quiet approach across the grass the figure literally jumped out of her skin at the sound of her voice. She turned, let out a loud high-pitched wail and leapt into the arms of the unsuspecting policewoman.

They both collapsed into a heap on the grass. Cole was submerged under a mass of wobbly flesh that was encased in a white chefs jacket, grey slacks and a voluminous blue and white striped apron.

"Holy Mary, Mother of God, pray for us sinners, now and at the hour of our death," howled the prostrate pastry provider. She then, after a slight pause, remembered to add "Amen" before continuing to wail.

Gathering his courage Day, with the help of Ball, who had eventually ventured further on to the lawn, managed to rescue Cole.

Having brushed themselves down they all stood in a circle looking at each other.

"Who are you?" snapped a still irritable Cole at the obviously Catholic cook before her.

"She's Mrs Breda Wilkins, our relief cook," answered Smallman before the still sobbing caterer could utter a word.

"Okay, Mrs Wilkins, what's all the fuss about? You made enough noise to wake the dead!" enquired Cole.

Those final words were the last straw and with a wail befitting the Hound of the Baskervilles, Breda Wilkins rotated her round body and pointed a podgy finger in the direction of the lightly steaming compost heap.

Smallman, Ball, Cole and Day stood open-mouthed. Like four statues they stared in stunned shocked horror before PC Day plummeted backwards to the ground.

Right in the centre of the compost heap sat Otto. In his mouth, reaching out as though desperate to escape was a substantially decayed, maggot-infested hand. From its bony fingers dog saliva dripped in glutinous globules onto the assorted vegetable matter below.

"I only came to... get rid of the peelings," bleated Wilkins.

"I found the hound and that," she paused staring once again in mute horror at the sight before her.

"What's the dog doing on there anyway?" enquired Ball who had now appeared to regain his composure.

"I thought Clive was supposed to be looking after it while Mrs Langton is, how you say, indisposed."

He hesitated then added, "How long has it been out here? I mean to consume a whole body, surely?"

"Don't be so stupid, Donald," rasped Smallman with such venom that Otto stopped chewing, dropped the hand and retreated whimpering, tail between legs into the furthest recess of the heap. "Have you seen the size of the dog? If anything looks like it's consumed a fully grown human it's her!" she snapped, pointing a bony finger in the direction of Breda Wilkins. The cook, oblivious to the barbed comments, continued to stare at the compost heap and its grisly contents.

"I say, dear," interjected Ball. "That's a little harsh."

"Look, Donald, call me fatist if you wish, but if the corpse fits, eat it, my mother always used to say."

"What was she, a cannibal?" sniped Cole. Then, quickly remembering her professional role in proceedings, began to take control of the situation. In order to avoid a further fainting fit, a pale PC Day, now upright and showing signs of recovery, was given the task of escorting Wilkins, Smallman and Ball back to the Manor to take statements.

As Cole observed the four figures retreating in the direction of the house a semblance of calm returned to the garden. She called the station and arranged with Sergeant Robson for the necessary backup and scenes of crime officers to attend the scene. Next she then turned her attention to Otto whose confidence had now returned. Gazing at the salivating mutt as it devoured yet another mouthful of evidence, Cole reflected on the fact that she had never owned a dog. Well not technically. Recently she had, for a short period of time, been left in charge of her parents' dachshund named Brandy, the experience being an episode in her life that she had tried hard to forget.

Brandy, or Randy as Cole chose to christen him, had an insatiable desire to mate with her 100% pure silk, hand-woven cushions. It was an unfortunate urge that did not endear him to her. This, coupled with the fact that he was an aggressively dominant dog who in the two days he was resident in her small town house kept her a virtual prisoner in the bedroom, meant his stay was not a relaxing one. During this forty-eight hour period her only means of escape was to distract him by throwing doggie chocs down the hall. Sadly, as Cole often found was the case in her life, the affair had ended badly. An over enthusiastic throw followed by a single-minded chase via footstool, chair and open window left Brandy airborne. She grimaced as she remembered the consequences of a sausage dog hitting the pavement fifteen feet below. Telling her parents that their standard pride and joy was now a miniature had been a very difficult task.

WPC Cole shook her head to vanquish the memories and re-focused on the problem in hand.

Over the next half an hour she tried an assortment of tricks to coax a possessive Otto from his feast. But all to no avail. She was still talking to the dog as though it were a two-month-old child when O'Brien appeared behind her. He assessed the situation in an instant and hurled a handful of gravel from the drive at the startled dog. Otto leapt from the compost heap with one bloodied finger bone poking out of the side of his mouth and lay down in comparative safety amongst the fruit trees.

DI Fricker sauntered across the lawn and joined O'Brien and Cole. He had a distracted look, his mind more focused on the forthcoming meeting with his mystery caller than the amputated appendage. It was now five to four, *only three hours to go*, he thought, and yet still he could not identify the female at the end of the phone.

"What's the problem, WPC Cole?" he asked as he glanced in the direction of the dribbling Doberman.

Cole spent fifteen minutes relating the events of the afternoon to her superiors and the following twenty endeavouring to entice Otto into the back of a police car. In the meantime the ubiquitous white police tent had been erected over the compost heap while an assortment of white-suited scenes of crime officers flitted in and out of the entrance like a small swarm of worker bees. Dr Body, who had dealt with more corpses in the last few days than he had in the whole of his career, was beginning to revel in the excitement of excavating the remains. A long white table ran along the back wall of the tent. On the top of the table, in a series of stainless steel bowls were an assortment of body parts in advanced stages of decay. The doctor was striding up and down cataloguing his finds when DI Fricker entered the tent.

"What news, Dr B? Any idea who, what, where or when?"

"Well, Giles, I've a femur, an ulna, five proximal phalanges, several putrid organs and this," he said brandishing a five-inch long red and brown tubular object.

"Well done, Doc, you're a genius; at least we know now it must have been a man," stated a relieved Fricker.

"You're right, Giles—" began the doctor.

"Put your glasses on, Dr Body," interjected O'Brien who had entered the tent unnoticed. "That, my learned friend, is a carrot!"

"I knew that, Sergeant," blustered Fricker and Body in unison as the former, flushing in embarrassment, turned on his heels and stormed outside. The latter unfazed by what he saw as a genuine mistake continued to sort his finds.

Stifling a smirk O'Brien addressed the doctor. "Let me know as soon as you've completed the jigsaw, Doc." Dr Body nodded acquiescingly in O'Brien's direction as the sergeant followed his superior out on to the lawn.

"I've a lot on my mind, O'Brien, I'm going back to the office and I've a, um, uh, meeting later. You deal with this, keep your eye on the vicar and let me know what you find out tomorrow," muttered Fricker who without waiting for a reply walked over to his car.

O'Brien sighed in mild exasperation and then, as had often been the case at a time of crisis, he watched his superior disappear and turned his attention to dealing with the mess.

CHAPTER 29

The Church of the Immaculate Conception stood on a corner, set back behind immaculately manicured lawns at the junction of Priory Lane and the main road into Hampton le Heath. A casually dressed Fricker had arrived early; he had taken the bus to avoid any passers-by recognising the unmarked police car he still used in the absence of his beloved Colin. The church was of a modern construction. It had a single spire, which would have resembled a fire station practice tower had it not been topped with a plain wooden cross. To the rear was a large un-ornate red brick, apex roofed hall, fronted by an unimposing small, covered entrance. From his vantage point behind a tall privet hedge on the other side of the road Fricker could observe the two streets. Seeing them empty of pedestrians and traffic he ran across, down the slab drive and into the porch. A sharp tug on the handle confirmed that the wooden doors were unlocked and after a moment's hesitation Fricker pulled them open and slid into the shadowy interior. An unadorned wooden screen obscured the main body of the church; Fricker pressed his ear to its surface and listened for any sign of activity within the building. As all seemed to be quiet he peered round the end of the screen into the open plan nave and up towards the altar. A burning candle, which Fricker recognised, from somewhere within the recesses of his mind, as a tabernacle light, was standing on the high altar. It flickered as though wafted by an unseen hand and the hairs on the back of his neck stood up as a cold chill ran down his spine.

Churches and Giles Fricker are not compatible, he thought.

Cautiously and nervously he made his way past the altar and up to the sacristy. There were two doors, one either side of the church. As it was closer he opened the one on the left and entered a small narrow room that stretched across the rear wall of the building. Peering through the gloom Fricker saw a number of robes and other garments hanging from a rail. He looked further and could just make out a small white sink in the corner. Beside this was a shelf containing an assortment of jugs, glasses and vases. Against the sink were propped a pair of bronze crosses on long wooden poles. Fricker glanced at his watch; it was five past seven. He was thinking how perceptive he had been to purchase one with luminous hands when he heard the front door of the church slam shut and the sound of shuffling feet travelling down the central aisle.

He moved as carefully and quietly as he could towards the door and was about to pull it open when he heard not one but two female voices. A surprised Fricker craned his neck to listen.

"How you know I was here?" bleated a foreign voice.

"Do you think I am stupid? I knew I could not trust you. It was obvious all I had to do was monitor your facebook and follow you. I told you before! Irritate him, embarrass him in the paper, but did I once tell you to blackmail him, you dim dago?" rasped the second voice.

"Sorry, what did you say? I am not a dago! I am Spanish," came the affronted reply. "I did as you tell me. I got the Insector—"

"Inspector, you fool!" interjected the second.

Fricker leaned further towards the door and gently attempted to open it in order to get a view of the two protagonists. A sharp squeak from the hinges soon made him stop.

The first voice continued.

"I want, I need the money… the amount you gave me do not cover my rent. I thought this was—"

"The problem is that you thought!"

There was a brief silence then she continued. "Listen to me, you inadequate dwarf! You do as I say, get him off the case, but do not let him know you are involved!"

"You no understand, I need a the money," whined the Spanish voice before she stopped abruptly. There was the noise of a scuffle and a guttural choking sound followed by a series of words so harshly delivered they made Fricker step back in fear.

"Look here, Dominguez! You do as I say or I'll kill your dog and if you haven't got a dog I'll kill your family and if you haven't got a family, which is more than likely, you deformed bastard, I'll kill you! Understand?"

Before the invisible victim could reply, realisation dawned on Fricker. It's the reporter!

Without thinking he shouted out loud, "It's the bloody Spanish reporter!"

Silence enveloped the church. Fricker moved back towards the door and was attempting to open it fully when his foot caught the outstretched pole of a processional cross. With enough noise to wake the dead he fell headlong through the opening and ended up nose first against the cold stone base of the altar.

As he shook his head to restore his blurred vision he heard the sound of footsteps running up the aisle. Looking up he was just in time to see the unmistakable figure of Jessica Garcia Aldoraz Dominguez, reporter from the *Evening Argos*, vanishing behind the screen at the far end of the nave. Her disappearance was followed shortly by the sound of the main door slamming shut.

So, Giles, you know the identity of the mysterious caller, he thought, *but who on earth was the other woman?*

By the time Fricker had stood up, made his way along the nave and exited the church, the street outside was devoid of any pedestrians. He scanned both ways and glanced at his watch. It was six minutes to eight, the light was beginning to dim and a light drizzle was beginning to fall.

The DI pondered for a few seconds more and then, satisfied that the reporter and her mysterious assailant had left the area, he began to cross the road towards the bus stop. He had almost reached halfway, immersed in his thoughts, when without warning a vehicle appeared out of nowhere along Priory Lane. Fricker was taken completely by surprise with the speed of the car and only just managed to leap to one side as it flew past, within inches of his flailing form. Eyes closed tightly he rolled like a half-empty barrel to the side of the road.

By the time he had recovered his equilibrium, brushed the remains of a recent roadkill from his corduroys and clambered to his feet the car was no longer in sight.

An hour later Fricker was sitting in his kitchen supping a large mug of hot chocolate. He was still feeling a little shaky and more than a little confused by the evening's events. In an attempt to clear his mind he randomly selected channels on the television. It was fruitless; he just could not concentrate.

He had no idea of the make or colour of the car involved, or who was driving and had therefore not reported the near miss to the station.

So, he pondered, *I now know the wretched reporter is out to get me, probably because I nearly ran her over at the funeral, but why do they want me off the case? Too many questions and not enough answers,* he thought and after what seemed an age a very sleepy DI Fricker decided that he would leave his decision making until the morning.

Nevertheless as he lay in his bed, he could not, however hard he tried, remove the niggling idea that he had heard the first woman's voice somewhere before.

The following morning Fricker was up early. His battered, aching, unfit body feeling the aftereffects of its close encounter with the tarmac. The weather did little to lift his air of gloom either. The blustery north wind scattered the clouds across the sky, unleashing at regular intervals their cargo of unseasonable squally, cold rain on the inhabitants of Hampton le Heath. By the time he had reached the station his grey Macintosh was sodden and the acid look he cast in the direction of Sergeant Robson sent the portly policeman scurrying down below the lip of his desk.

Five minutes later there was a firm knock on his office door.

"Yes!" snapped Fricker.

An annoyingly cheerful O'Brien breezed into the room, sat down opposite his DI and deposited a pile of notes on the desk.

"Good morning, sir."

"Good? I can think of nothing that is good about this miserable morning," replied Fricker. "What have you got to report from yesterday?"

"Right, sir. The compost heap has been completely excavated. Doctor Body worked all night; he was like a man possessed. He has identified one hundred and eighty-four bones out of two hundred and six. We're missing two ribs and twenty hand bones that we believe the dog has eaten, but other than that we have a full house."

Fricker looked quizzically at his sergeant. "How long has the body been in the heap? I presume a long time as it was so well on its way to being completely decomposed?"

"Well, sir, this is where it gets interesting. It would appear that the corpse had been submerged and dissolved in acid, probably sodium hydroxide with water."

"Sodium what?" queried Fricker.

"Caustic soda, sir. Dr Body believes the deceased has been dead for less than three days and as we have a full set of teeth it will not be long before we identify who it is."

"Bloody hell, O'Brien!" shouted the DI as a wave of relief washed over him. "You mean to say that we might actually be making some progress at last?"

"Yes, sir, and that's not all, I was talking to Dr Body at the morgue and he suggested that whoever murdered Fanshaw and Maitland might suffer from dyscalculia."

Fricker stared blankly at his sergeant.

O'Brien, recognising his superior's all too familiar expression of incomprehension, proceeded to explain in simplistic terms the definition of dyscalculia and the reasons behind Dr Body's theory.

After a short pause to process the information Fricker replied in a dismissive tone.

"I see, O'Brien, an interesting hypothesis. That's the trouble with doctors and the like, always want to give people a label. Next thing he'll say is that his father was a campanol—" He stopped abruptly in mid-sentence.

A puzzled O'Brien was just about to ask the question when a relieved Fricker, having avoided an awkward moment, continued on a totally new track.

"How did the interviews go? Did you talk to the vicar? What happened to the dog?"

Fricker and a perplexed O'Brien spent the next hour discussing the questions. In general the answers were that none of the people questioned by PC Day and subsequently by O'Brien had any idea who the body was and how it came to be in the centre of the compost heap. With regard to Otto, he, after much coaxing, was now safely in the pound. This was not really the response a morose Fricker was hoping for. In his mind Ball was still at the top of his list of suspects.

The conversation, having started to rotate in circles, was dying a death and Fricker took the opportunity to confide in his sergeant about the dramatic events of the previous evening.

O'Brien listened intently. For once he agreed with his superior that it would probably have not been a good idea to arrest Aldoraz Dominguez as they had no proof that it was her driving the car. More importantly as far as Fricker was concerned he could not risk a third bout of adverse publicity. After all, she still had the photo from the Pagoda Dragon.

There were two further questions that continued to cause both O'Brien and Fricker concern. Who was the mystery woman in the church and, albeit for totally differing reasons, why would she want him off the case?

The two senior officers were still pondering the whys and wherefores of the investigation when the door to the office was forcefully swung open and a flustered-looking WPC Cole barged in. She stood to attention by the door. Fricker's heart skipped a beat as he eyed the ample proportions of her bust and finely sculptured features of her face.

Forgetting for a moment that Sergeant O'Brien was still sitting opposite him he grinned broadly and in a voice reminiscent of Fagin he greeted the young WPC.

"Rita, my dear, how are you? You look if I may say, like a perfect angel."

O'Brien, amazed at the speed Fricker's mood fluctuated from one extreme to another, choked violently on his tea and biscuits.

Cole stood, open-mouthed, the colour draining from her puce face in an instant. *Oh God*, she thought, looking across the room at his leering expression, his lower lip once again drooping and salivating like an over-excited bloodhound. *What should I do now?*

As usual in times of stress and particularly when in close contact with her superior her mind went in to overload. Her cerebral cortex scanned its deepest recess for any obscure dictionary definition that would put him off his obvious train of thought. Sadly though she quickly concluded there was no alternative. He meant what he said. He perceived her as being entirely without any flaws, defects or shortcomings, having the qualities of an angel: beauty, purity or kindliness and there was no way she could persuade him otherwise.

"Oh, er, thank you, sir, you too," she babbled and then to avoid any additional embarrassment she continued to talk at speed.

"The Doc Body has teeth, knows who body is see, sir—"

"Get a grip, Cole," snapped O'Brien so sharply that both Cole and Fricker stood silently to attention.

"Whoops, sorry, Sarge," she muttered.

After a moment's hesitation she continued. "What I meant to say was that Dr Body has identified the compost corpse, sir."

"Well yes, come on, Cole, who is it?" probed an irritated O'Brien as Fricker continued to leer across the desk at the uncomfortable WPC.

"Well sir, it would appear that the body belongs to Margaret Bronwyn-Jones, also known as Martin I believe."

"So that's where she's been hiding," said Fricker absentmindedly.

"And what's more, sir," continued Cole, "having trawled through her medical records it would appear that she was about to undergo sex realignment."

"Sex what?" queried a perplexed Fricker.

"Sex realignment, sir, it's when the—"

"Spare the details, WPC," interjected O'Brien. "Was there anything else in the records?"

"Um, no, I don't think so, Sarge," she said glancing down at her notebook. "Oh yes, sorry, Sarge, she had piles and was, I'm not sure how you pronounce it... dicks calckulick?"

"Dyscalculia, Cole, dyscalculia. Well I'll be a monkey's uncle, the murdering Welsh culinary cutthroat did it, she killed Maitland and Fanshaw!" roared O'Brien.

"And then she committed suicide I presume, case solved. Well done, team," stated a beaming Fricker who then added, "I always knew it couldn't have been the vicar."

Carried away with the euphoria of the moment O'Brien was just about to agree with his superior when the stupidity of Fricker's last but one statement dawned on him.

"Suicide, sir? How could she have dissolved herself in a bath of acid, then got out, carried her bones to the vegetable garden and buried herself in the compost heap?"

WPC Cole, who had remained standing by the door, sniggered, then looked down and studied her pocket book.

"Don't be so pedantic, O'Brien, she might have had an accomplice," snapped Fricker and after a slight pause added, "the vicar maybe!"

O'Brien emitted a long sigh of despair, but before he could reply, a grinning WPC Cole interrupted.

"There was one other thing, sir."

"What is it, Rita?" simpered the DI.

The constable read from her notes. "Dr Body said the cause of death was a sharp wound to the back of the head that penetrated the skull and would have caused severe trauma to the brain. He had to say 'would have', sir, as we haven't got a brain to examine as it was dissolved in the acid. Dr Body also said that the diameter of the weapon at the point of entry was slightly less than half an inch. Similar to a stiletto, sir."

Fricker frowned and buried his head in his hands.

"So, sir, looks like we've got a second murderer on our hands; shall I get the ball rolling on this new enquiry?" stated O'Brien.

There was a short period of silence broken finally by a monosyllabic grunt. Taking this as approval for his course of action O'Brien gathered up his papers and ushered a relieved Cole out of the room.

CHAPTER 30

Hillary Smallman was on a mission. Following the previous day's arrival of Constables Cole and Day and the subsequent discovery of the body in the heap, she had gone into organisational overdrive. *Donald Ball was no use*, she thought. He had retreated into his shell after being interviewed yet again. Despite several attempts to cajole, persuade and abuse him in to action he had decamped to his office and immersed himself in *The House at Pooh Corner*. Her relief cook was still in a state of shock and the inmates of Scotswood Manor were becoming very restless, not to mention hungry.

A series of deputations had arrived at her door over the last twelve hours. They first had requested, then demanded, dinner and breakfast and would, before long she expected, require tea. The ringleaders, as Smallman saw it, were Edna and her weak sidekick Hilda along with the wretched Nixdorf woman; the latter she had observed was, with her Queen Victoria morning apparel, playing the grieving-friend card far too much.

Smallman had given them what they wanted in a fashion. Her cooking skills left a lot to be desired, but, at the end of the day, the consequences of a bout of food poisoning would only mean another room to fill from Scotswood's ever expanding waiting list. *It was funny*, she mused, *how the appearance of a mass murderer at a care home and the possibility of further deaths brought in so many greedy relatives and their befuddled charges.*

Help was at a premium for Smallman; with Langton on bail and convalescing at her sister's in Sidcup, Bronwyn-Jones dead as a dodo and Breda Wilkins still recovering from her ordeal, Clive was her one remaining functional member of staff.

The horde of policemen wandering the grounds did not help matters either, she thought. The last thing she wanted was a further bout of questioning from the inadequate DI or his effeminate PC. The arrival, therefore, of WPC Cole at the already open front door irritated her, to say the least.

Mop bucket in hand and hair tied up in a faded tartan headscarf she had just descended the stairs having cleaned the attic rooms, when Cole entered the hallway.

"Ah, Miss Smallman, I'm glad I've caught you!"

Smallman looked like she had seen a ghost. The bucket crashed from her pale shaking hand and brown murky water cascaded in all directions across the hall's tiled floor. The water that didn't disappear through the gaps under the skirting boards to the cellar below lapped up against Cole's boots or remained, like a small lake, outside the office door.

"Shit! Caught me, why? What have I done?" she exclaimed while bent on one knee as she franticly attempted to mop up the remaining water.

Before Cole could reply, the door to the office slowly opened and the tired face of Donald Ball peeked out. He peered down at the figure kneeling on the floor.

"Um, Piglet, I presume, must have been a bad storm in the hundred acre wood, ha, ha," he said, then slowly closed the door.

As he disappeared Smallman shot him a look that, had he seen, would have turned him to stone. She then turned her attention towards Cole.

"Yes, what do you want? Can't you see I'm busy?"

Cole wasn't in the mood to take prisoners either. After her escape from the DI's office, Sergeant O'Brien had vented his frustrations regarding his superior's attitude on anyone within hearing. Cole had been firmly in the firing line. Having finished berating her, O'Brien had then despatched the quivering WPC to the Manor. His final instruction to her still echoed around her head: "Squeeze Smallman and Ball until their pips squeak!"

"Look here," Cole rasped. "I'm getting more than a little tired of your unhelpful, evasive and downright rude ways. I will ask the questions and you, Miss Smallman, will answer them! Understand?"

Having mopped the floor as well as she could Smallman got to her feet and looked up at the WPC.

"Yes, if I must," she said. "What is it you want?"

"That's better, Miss Smallman," retorted Cole. "A little uptight, aren't we?"

"I'm under a lot of stress at the moment, Officer Cole, I'm sorry if I was a little short with you. Seriously how can I help you?" she replied, her face breaking into a semblance of a smile.

Cole mellowed slightly. She could see from the deep lines and dark circles around Smallman's eyes that she must not have been sleeping well.

"Well, Miss Smallman, there are a couple of things I would like to ask you."

Smallman peered intently at Cole, then gesturing with her arm invited the WPC into the lounge.

They both sat down in the high-backed, winged, chintz armchairs and Cole got out her police issue notebook.

CHAPTER 31

With O'Brien, Day and Cole all otherwise engaged, Fricker once again sat back in his chair and began to contemplate life. The previous night's events, the announcement that the cook had been composted and the fact that there definitely was another murderer on the loose all swirled around his mind. The concoction of information surged around like a whirlpool and at the centre, peeking out at regular intervals, was a vision of his beloved WPC Cole. With his eyes closed he looked, to any casual observer, as though he had gone quite insane. His demeanour alternated between confusion and contentment until the shrill ring of the telephone shattered his peace.

Five minutes later Fricker sat at his desk, the telephone receiver still clutched in his hand as he pondered the two calls he had received in quick succession. The first, from Aldoraz Dominguez, was not unexpected. He knew that eventually she would want to speak to him having missed the opportunity at the church. However, the second call, from Pauline Petrie, was a surprise. Having heard nothing from her since the ill-fated night at the Pagoda Dragon he sadly thought that perhaps that had been the end of their fledgling relationship. With Cole playing hard to get, it would have been good to have more than one iron in the fire. At least that was what his latest 'how to date' self-help book had advocated.

Initially when Pauline had called he sensed a little spark in her voice, he even felt, albeit briefly, that there really might be something between them; but then when he had mentioned the wretched Spanish reporter, well, it was as though he had made some very inappropriate joke.

From that point on the atmosphere had the warmth of an icicle in Siberia. When he had casually stated that he was to meet Dominguez again, this time at the disused canal basin on the far side of town, Pauline had slammed the phone down with such vigour it had made his eyes water.

Jealousy, he mused, *that's all it can be, the feisty minx is jealous.* A contented grin settled on Fricker's face as he turned his thoughts to the reporter and once again tried to work out what she was after. The overheard conversation at the church intimated that someone wanted DI Fricker off the case, but the Spaniard only seemed interested in money. *There was only one thing for it*, he mused: *confront the woman and deal with her for good.*

Meanwhile at Scotswood Manor the mood in the lounge was tense. WPC Cole had spent an hour going over Smallman's various statements. Despite her intense grilling the WPC had to concede that Smallman's alibis were watertight. With the exception of making more room for residents she had no obvious reason to kill any of the three victims. It was, however, when Cole again quizzed her on the activity in the attic rooms that she encountered, what she perceived to be, an evasive attitude.

"Look, Miss Smallman," she continued, trying hard to adopt a more understanding tone. "I know that the lights in the attic rooms have been on at all hours of the day. All I am asking you is why? Surely that can't be too hard a question." She paused, then added, "Unless you have something to hide?"

Hillary Smallman's eyes darted from one corner of the room to the other, never stopping to rest and never focusing on WPC Cole either as she franticly fumbled with her cuffs.

"Well, it's like this, Constable," she mumbled "It's—"

Her words were cut short by an enormously loud crashing

sound. This was followed by a howl of anguished pain that seemed to emanate from the room above the lounge.

"What on earth was that?" shouted Cole trying hard to be heard above the still reverberating noise.

"It sounds like the bloody Nixdorf woman," barked Smallman.

Simultaneously they jumped to their feet, ran head down through the door and bumped straight into Sergeant O'Brien and PC Day.

"What the hell is wrong with this place today?" snapped O'Brien as he picked Smallman up from the floor.

"We just met Tigger in reception, are deafened by that and assaulted by you!"

"Sorry, Sarge," bleated Cole. "We were just on our way to investigate the…"

She stopped in mid-sentence while all four stood still, listening intently as the clamour above continued unabated.

To O'Brien's surprise it was Day who reacted first. Having glanced sideways at the mirror on the hall wall, adjusted his helmet and admired his profile, he skipped across the tiled floor and ascended the stairs two at a time.

After a moment's hesitation, O'Brien, Cole and Smallman followed. The noise of the four as they charged up the stairs mixed with the yet to be identified tormented wailing was enough even to raise the soporific residents of Scotswood. The opening of doors, shuffling of swollen, slippered feet and toothless chatter added to the cacophony of sound.

O'Brien, fuelled by military pride and superior fitness, surged past PC Day on the final bend of the stairs.

However, as he rounded the corner onto the landing he came to a sudden stop.

"What the—!"

His three companions, who almost colliding with him as they blindly followed his lead, just managed to stop in time and peered over and around his shoulders. Before them, almost completely obscuring the entrance to the room at the end of the corridor was the enormous bulk that was Martha Nixdorf.

She was lying face down across the floor like a beached whale. Her small dumpy feet waggling in the air and her arms rotating in violent anger as she pummelled an unseen victim beneath her.

Nixdorf continued to shout and wail an assortment of colliery curses as her invisible prey moaned incoherently, muffled by the folds of flesh and crimplene that enveloped it.

Avoiding the discarded Zimmer frame O'Brien and Day moved forward and each grabbed a flailing arm. Cole peered and reached through the mass of soft tissue, seized a handful of superfluous fabric and lent her muscle to the effort. Meanwhile, Smallman seeing the opportunity to avoid further questioning turned around and silently crept back along the corridor, down the stairs and out of the front door.

After five minutes of struggling and oblivious to the departure of their suspect, the three officers finally managed to raise Martha Nixdorf to her feet. She stood unsteadily, supported by her Zimmer and the ever-helpful PC Day while O'Brien and Cole attended to the prone casualty.

"That's Edna!" exclaimed Cole.

"Fat Edna! Edna who?" retorted O'Brien, his hearing temporarily impaired by the previous wailing. He paused, peered at the pale, squashed, shallow breathing geriatric then continued. "If she was obese before, she certainly isn't now."

CHAPTER 32

DI Fricker glanced at his watch. It was three forty-five. *Fifteen minutes to go*, he thought as he sat in Colin at the far end of the car park. He was pleased that his beloved car had now been restored to its former glory, but mused to himself that this would not be the case for long if he had to negotiate many more pot hole strewn apologies for car parks such as this one.

The air was turning cold after the earlier rain. Fricker pulled up the collar of his sheepskin coat and huddled down in his seat to keep warm. He made a mental note that there were three other vehicles parked in the vicinity and as he certainly did not recognise any of them he presumed that they were dog walkers or the like.

He started to doze off, an aftereffect of his stressful week and was just in the process of emitting his first snore, when he was jolted awake by the slamming of a car door.

"What the!" Fricker exclaimed as his eyes scanned the parked cars for any signs of life. A movement to the rear of an old grey Fiat caught his attention and to his surprise the hobbling form of Clive, the handyman from Scotswood Manor, shuffled into view. He was carrying, with some difficulty, a large wicker basket and strung over his shoulder was a long canvas holdall.

Fricker shrank further down into his seat to avoid being seen and carefully watched as Clive slowly made his way up to the 'You are here' map. Resting on his stick, the overloaded caretaker hesitated for a few seconds, rotated his head a couple of times to get his bearings and then trundled off in the direction of the canal basin.

How strange, Fricker mused as he glanced at his watch. It was three fifty-five.

Fricker slowly and reluctantly extracted himself from the relatively snug comfort of Colin's interior. Having closed and locked the door he followed, head down and collar up, in the direction recently taken by Clive.

He had only travelled about ten yards when, with his eyes firmly focused on the ground in front of him, he walked straight into a small man coming in the opposite direction.

"What, who are, sorry," blustered Fricker as he staggered backwards as a result of the collision. The other man peered up at Fricker, almost impervious to the force of their encounter.

"Ho, terribly sorry sir," he said and then with a dim light of recognition in his narrow eyes he continued "Oh Mr Icker, we meet again. I did not realise it was you. You look a little different sober."

Fricker was taken aback. *What the hell was Mr Chow doing there?* he thought as he looked down at the Chinaman who was dressed in a black hoody and black jeans.

"Ah so, Mr Chow! What brings you here?"

"Oh you know, sir," Chow began, then after a moment's hesitation continued; "I was looking for some rainbow trout for… for the chef's special. Must go."

As Fricker mulled over his reply the inscrutable black-clad oriental swiftly side-stepped past and disappeared into the gloomy, tree shadowed car park.

Strange, very strange, mused Fricker.

He glanced once more in the direction taken by Chow.

Having seen that there were no further signs of activity Fricker continued along the road towards the canal basin.

He had travelled a further twenty yards when he heard the sound of a car engine start up somewhere behind him. Assuming this to be Mr Chow he ignored the noise of the approaching vehicle and carried on his way.

The clamour of the car engine mixed with the sound of displaced gravel and spinning wheels grew increasingly louder. Fricker turned around in alarm.

He was just in time, as for the second time in a couple of days he found himself the target of a hit and run driver. Instinctively Fricker dived for the safety of the hedge that bordered the rock-strewn drive, the dark-coloured motor just missed his flailing feet by a matter of inches, veered sharply to avoid the edge of the canal bank and without stopping disappeared in a plume of dust out on to the main road.

Fricker lay, bruised and scratched but otherwise uninjured, in the base of a laurel and holly hedge. He sniffed the air and found that he was surrounded and, as he suspected, immersed in the remains of several discarded dog faeces collection bags. He fought hard to control the urge to retch as, much to his disgust, he discovered that their foul smelling contents were already smeared across the smooth fawn contours of his sheepskin coat.

"Shit!" he exclaimed. "That bloody Chow, he'll swing for this."

Further expletives followed as he endeavoured to extract himself from the hedge when two short but powerful arms grabbed him from behind and pulled him to his feet.

Fricker turned abruptly and found he was once again looking down into the oriental eyes of Mr Chow.

"You alright, Mr Icker? I saw it happen, lousy driver, must be woman!" he exclaimed.

A dazed Fricker could only nod and stare in confused disbelief. It if hadn't been Chow, then who had it been?

He pondered the matter with some difficulty.

"What colour was the car, Mr Chow?" he asked, then continued without waiting for a reply. "Did you get a look at its number plate?"

An inscrutable smile swept slowly across the Chinaman's face.

Regaining a little of his composure and resigned to the fact that he would not get any further comment, Fricker sighed and turned away.

He walked for a few paces, then stopped and after a moment's hesitation, gingerly unearthed his slightly battered phone from the pocket of his coat and dialled the station.

Having instructed PC Day to mobilise some backup in the form of himself, Sergeant O'Brien and WPC Cole, Fricker made his way cautiously towards the canal basin. The tree-lined pathway that led away from the car park was eerily silent. There was no sign of Clive, and Chow, having walked off in the opposite direction, had left in his car shortly after their meeting.

The whole thing gets stranger and stranger, mused Fricker as he contemplated the murders, attempts on his life and strange goings-on at Scotswood Manor. There seemed to be no factor linking the whole series of events. He more or less knew who had killed Maitland and Fanshaw, but who had killed Bronwyn-Jones? "The Spaniard!" he shouted out loud as he remembered the reason why he was wandering along the edge of the canal basin. Perhaps she had been involved?

The thought spurred him on and obliterated all memories of his recent brush with death. He ignored the still all-pervasive smell from his coat and strode purposefully along the path.

Two minutes later he reached the main area of the basin. The canal widened and a series of decaying, disused red brick warehouses lined the edge. Fricker looked up and took in the scene. He shuddered in his sheepskin. The whole area, he felt, oozed a sense of foreboding. Dark rain clouds scudded across the sky and the height of the buildings cast vast shadows over the already sun-starved water.

In the far corner Fricker could just make out the hunched figure of a man sitting on a basket and staring intently into the black murky canal.

After several seconds thought, Fricker deduced it must be Clive. He had never considered that he might be a closet fisherman; *but on reflection*, he mused, *his morose, anti-social demeanour was a bit of a giveaway.*

There was, however, no sign of Aldoraz Dominguez.

Where the hell was the woman? Fricker snapped inwardly as he continued to scan the area for signs of life.

Everywhere was bleak; all the warehouse doors appeared to be boarded up, metal riveted plates festooned every entrance and window opening whilst unintelligible graffiti blanketed the crumbling brickwork.

"Are you okay, sir?" shouted PC Day as he approached along the canal path.

Fricker turned around abruptly. "Oh, Day! I never heard you. Yes, I'm fine now."

Sergeant O'Brien and WPC Cole appeared around the corner and quickly joined their colleague who had stopped abruptly five yards or so from his superior.

"Whoa! What is that smell, sir?" enquired O'Brien, who then found it hard to hide a smirk as he subdued the urge to ask whether or not it was yet another new aftershave.

Cole and Day had both turned away, fingers pinched tightly over noses while an embarrassed DI Fricker endeavoured to explain the pungent aroma that emanated from his clothing.

Explanation over and seemingly oblivious to his colleagues' continuing discomfort, he began to relate the tale of his close brush with death. Gesticulating wildly with his arms to indicate various parts of the action only served to spread the vile smell further along the canal path.

Looking around for a means of escape O'Brien's eyes focused on the figure of Clive, bent intently over his fishing rod.

"That's Clive from the Manor if I'm not mistaken," stated O'Brien who then proposed, much to the relief of Day and Cole, that DI Fricker wait where he was while they all went and had a word with him.

Without waiting for a reply, all three squeezed past Fricker as quickly as they could and walked swiftly towards the handyman who by now was struggling with an object of some size on the end of his line.

The closer they got the clearer it became that Clive had hooked a monster.

"What you got there then, Moby Dick?" laughed O'Brien.

A startled Clive swung round on his one good leg and almost overbalanced, losing control of his tackle in the process.

"What... oh, it's you," he muttered then in an instant turned his attention to his rod, which by now was almost bent double.

For a few moments he strained and pulled against the invisible but immovable entity. Realising he could not win the unequal battle he addressed O'Brien in a more conciliatory manner.

"Give us a hand, mate, I've never caught a pike this big here. It's a bloody whopper!"

O'Brien, Cole and Clive grabbed the oscillating pole whilst Day looked on, hands intertwined, fingers twisting in nervous excitement as he offered words of encouragement.

The murky water frothed and bubbled while the unseen object clung on to its freedom.

"Bloody obstinate thing, must be female," grunted Clive.

Cole glared in annoyance and gave an Amazonian heave on the rod.

Instantly the tension on the line reduced. All three staggered backwards, in the process knocking Day sideward into the hedgerow.

Recovering his composure O'Brien followed the route of the line and scanned the dirty black agitated water.

He had just begun to mouth, "Looks like it got away" when from the depths of the canal basin appeared the weed-festooned face of a woman.

Day, having extracted himself from the hedgerow, promptly fainted, Clive vomited, and Cole turned aside in revulsion. O'Brien, however, stared in absorbed disgust at the sight before them.

"Good God, she's ugly," mused Fricker who, having discarded his sheepskin coat and masked by the smell of mud from the bottom of the basin, had made his way, nasally unheralded, to join them.

Ignoring the suffering of their subordinates and Clive, Fricker and O'Brien viewed the newly released corpse as it bobbed up and down on the surface of the water.

A mixture of slime and weed partially obscured the face.

Day, now used to fainting, had recovered quickly and was now standing beside them, his pale face staring into the water.

"Who do you think it is, sir?"

Fricker peered intently. "The nose is very prominent and the body quite short."

He sighed, a clear indication to those around him that the grey cells were a little distracted and needed a bit more time.

"I was supposed to meet that reporter, you know Miss Dominguez from the *Evening Argos*. It could be her, the nose is similar—"

"Shouldn't we get her out, sir? Before she sinks," interjected Cole.

"Hmm," responded Fricker.

Taking that for a yes, O'Brien and Cole requisitioned Clive's rod and after several attempts managed to hook the body and pull it onto the bank.

Wrapped around the corpse's head was a large object that oozed water as it was dragged out of the canal.

Fricker bent down for a closer look.

"Yes, I think I'm right it's—"

"Yes, sir, by God you are," interjected PC Day. "it's a designer bag and if I'm not mistaken a very expensive bag! If I'm also not mistaken it's the floral bouquet extra large print design!"

"Wow, I've always wanted that one," gushed Cole.

O'Brien, head in hands, sighed in disgust. Day and Cole were just poised to continue the impromptu meeting of the fashion accessory appreciation society when they were interrupted.

"Oh my God, I know who that is," blurted out the slightly stuttering voice of Clive.

Fricker, Cole, Day and O'Brien turned towards him in silence.

"It's my boss, it's that bloody old bat, Smallman."

CHAPTER 33

Donald S Ball was sitting in his office slumped at his desk. His bottom lip wobbled as tears streamed down his sunken cheeks, dripping silently onto the stuffed toy he cradled in his arms.

"For God's sake, Mr Ball, get a grip. Stop blabbing and put the wretched bear down," snapped O'Brien.

He could appreciate him being upset, but it was now an hour after he and Cole had broken the news of Hillary Smallman's death and still he hadn't uttered a coherent word.

"You, you don't understand. She was my rock."

O'Brien stifled a smile. *He's more right than he thinks; after all she certainly sank like a stone, but,* he reflected, *who wouldn't with a bag that size wrapped around their neck.*

"We know this is distressing, Mr Ball, but we need to know when did you last see Hillary and why was she at the canal basin?" asked WPC Cole in an effort to change the style of questioning.

"She was my rock," he repeated.

O'Brien and Cole looked at each other. They knew it was going to be a very long night.

The following morning, Giles Fricker was at Headquarters, sitting uncomfortably on a now all too familiar hard wooden chair in an all too familiar office.

Across the desk sat Chief Constable Godfrey Hogarth.

"If there's one thing I hate more than a murder, Fricker, it's—"

"Three murders?"

"No, you blithering idiot!"

Fricker gasped at the harshness in his superior's tone.

"What I hate, DI Fricker, is scandal and you've had more than your share of scandal over the past week."

Hogarth's facial colour fluctuated like a traffic light as he proceeded to berate Fricker for his lack of progress on the four murder investigations and his overall handling of the kidnapping of PC Day. The tirade lasted for what seemed to be an eternity as each pause, which Fricker perceived to be the end, turned out to be the beginning of further accusations of incompetent procedure and tactics.

Finally, Hogarth took what appeared to be a final long intake of breath.

Fricker sighed, prepared to emit his first syllable in response, but got no further than the 't' of thank you.

"What's more, Fricker!"

"More, sir?"

"What's more is that I have received an email."

Try as he might Fricker could not suppress a smirk. He was unable to subdue the image of a techno-phobic Hogarth, his one finger with the capability to type, moving like an inebriated slowworm across the keyboard.

"Something amusing you, Fricker?" barked Hogarth not waiting for an answer.

"Well then, laugh at this. The email states that you had the motive and opportunity to murder Miss Smallman. It goes on in some detail to outline your actions on the afternoon in question and leaves me with many worrying questions!"

"Ha, ha," giggled the now pale Detective Inspector. "It must be a joke... surely?"

"No joke, Fricker, and it leaves me only one option... you're suspended on full pay until this is resolved and should you come anywhere near your team or this case, I'll have you incarcerated before you can say Jack Bennett!"

Now ashen, the shell-shocked Fricker considered correcting his superior, but declined this inclination as he took in the enormity of his dire predicament.

An hour later O'Brien, Cole and Day were standing silently outside DI Fricker's office. There was no sign of life from behind the closed door.

"That's strange," commented Cole. "You can usually hear him talking to himself at least."

Her colleagues grunted in agreement. It had been a long night following the latest grizzly discovery and after a long and fruitless interview with Ball no one had managed any meaningful sleep.

They continued their silent vigil for a further five minutes until the relative tranquillity of the landing was shattered by the echoed pounding of size nine police boots from the concrete footwell below.

Six eyes swivelled in the direction of the noise.

Six eyebrows were raised as the shabbily uniformed figure of Sergeant Robson appeared, flustered, worn out and perspiring heavily.

Day, O'Brien and Cole all took a step back. Robson came to a halt, huffing, puffing and salivating like an out of condition spaniel. He paused, took a deep breath and began to speak.

"DI Fricker... he's been... by the CC!"

"He's been what by the CC?" snapped O'Brien.

"DI Fricker, um, he has been suspended!"

"Suspended!"

"Yes, suspended by Mr Hogarth."

PC Day stumbled backwards against the wall, his head swimming on the verge of an all too familiar faint. *It can't be true*, he thought; the traumatic vision emblazoned on his mind of his idol hanging from Hogarth's office doorframe.

"You mean actually suspended?" he bleated, trying hard to stem the onset of tears.

"No, you blithering idiot," rasped O'Brien. "He means—"

WPC Cole interjected. "He means he's banned, debarred, exiled, frozen out, precluded, prevented from—"

"Stopped from working on this case and sent home," barked O'Brien in an attempt to restore some order to the conversation and end Cole's dictional drivel.

After a brief pause Robson, having recovered from his unaccustomed exercise, added some further detail to the story, explaining and elaborating on what he had heard third-hand from a dog handler who was based at HQ.

The landing descended into a hushed silence as they all took in the news.

"This can't be true, Sarge! The DI could never be a murderer, could he?" whined Day.

O'Brien sighed and looked around at the downcast group in front of him. *These were going to require a bit of motivation*, he thought. He puffed out his chest and trawled the recesses of his mind for a latent motivational speech from his military past.

"Look team, I've known DI Fricker for a number of years now. He may have his issues, but he's a good boss, most of the time at least, and he's not a killer. We've four murders on our hands and we are not going to let him down. So," he paused for effect. "Get your lacklustre arses into gear, let's find the killer, fight to clear DI Fricker's name and take no prisoners!"

Cole and Robson clapped enthusiastically while PC Day wiped a solitary tear from his cheek and stood trying hard to comprehend the final statement.

"Sorry, Sarge, but how can we find the killer but take no prisoners?"

The question fell on deaf ears as the other three had already dispersed; motivated, determined to right wrongs and bring justice to the streets of Hampton le Heath.

It was a different picture in Giles Fricker's house.

He stared mournfully at his two graduation pictures; the sun shining down on his sullen youthful face as, adorned by cap and gown, he posed alone in front of his university's laundrette, and in the later one, dressed in full uniform, standing sodden after torrential rain on the entrance steps of Bramshill Police College.

What could have gone so wrong? he mused. The vicar had done it he was certain; at least he had been certain at the start, then yesterday when Smallman had been dragged from the canal? It could have been Clive or Chow, but neither had been in the car that tried to run him down, so who was it and who had written the email? Hogarth had stated that it was sent anonymously from an internet café so no clues there. *Plenty of questions*, he thought, *but no answers.*

Fricker sunk his head in his hands. He had tried to ring Dr Schruff only to find he was on sabbatical in Bratislava and to make matters worse his severed rabbit's foot and putrefied Bockwurst sausage were still in his office desk drawer.

Restlessly he got up. Making his way to the window he paused and peered through the grime-laden pane at the rows of gardens that backed on to each other like cars in a car park. Fricker wasn't a gardener; his little plot of Eden resembled the Amazonian jungle rather than a suburban idyll.

He leant his head on his hands and reflected on a dire day and life in general.

Fricker had never been one to socialise with his neighbours; unsociable hours had not helped, but then neither had his insular disposition.

He absentmindedly scanned the gardens either side of his overgrown wilderness. Some days when he peered out of the upstairs window he quite expected to see a member of a long lost tribe or a second world war Japanese soldier emerge from the undergrowth of his own plot, grunting incoherently or crying "banzi… long live the Emperor."

The former seemed more appropriate as two figures appeared on the lawn to the right. Rose and Sandie were a funny couple; the exact nature of their relationship was, as far as Fricker was concerned, a little hard to fathom. *Not that this was a problem*, he mused to himself. He liked to think of himself as broad-minded, after all he had recently dealt with a deceased, decomposed transvestite so a little batting for the other side, if that were the case, was, in comparison, perfectly acceptable. The two ladies in question strolled arm in arm across the verdant sward of green between borders bathed in a profusion of spring flowers and shrubs. Fricker hardly knew a daffodil from a tulip, but was artistic enough to recognise a well-maintained garden. He smiled at the view, an emotion that in itself was a surprise, given the recent turn of events.

He continued to observe Rose and Sandie as they dawdled around their plot.

Sandie was a stocky lass, as Fricker's Uncle Albert would have described her. Although Albert would have gone further and added, good breeding stock, but that would not have been appropriate for this particular specimen. She was crested with short, spiky ginger hair and that afternoon, as was usually the case, wore a brown tweed trouser suit, a style that gave her a rather matronly look. *Big, intimidating and loud,* thought Fricker; another one who stirred up reminiscences of the dreadful Mrs Yates, a vision compounded by the fact she nurtured bluebells in profusion throughout her garden. *Given her size, Big Bertha bell peppers might have been more appropriate*, mused Fricker before turning his attention to her partner. Rose was slightly older, Fricker estimated, in her early fifties. Slender in comparison she was still on the dumpy side, but slightly shorter in height.

He continued to watch them. Their behaviour had taken on a more purposeful air as, from a pocket in Rose's flower-bedecked overall, she produced two pairs of bright gardening secateurs. Their blades glinted in the sunlight as Rose passed one pair to her partner and they both set about vigorously pruning a rampant patch of ivy that had had the audacity to attach itself to a small summerhouse in the corner of the lawn. The unpleasant profiles of both Rose and Sandie were soon out of sight as their blitz on the ivy continued to the rear of the building.

Fricker adjusted the direction of his gaze and began to study the garden to the left of his own.

Ignoring the state of his plot, a greater contrast between this piece of wasteland and that maintained by the gruesome twosome could not be imagined. Fricker often referred to the three gardens as the good, the bad and the ugly. The term ugly aptly described the domain of a family who Fricker classed as immobile travellers. Despite the logistical impossibility of the idea, he quite expected to see that half a dozen assorted nomadic dwellings had appeared on their back lawn each time he glanced in that direction. In addition Fricker used the word lawn euphemistically. In reality the patch of scorched earth consisted of a long brown mud path festooned with an array of discarded children's toys and old domestic appliances, topped with a bank of decaying wooden pet cages. These had, over the years, been the homes for a varied assortment of neglected furry animals including, to Fricker's knowledge at least, eight rabbits and four ferrets. The last of the latter he had nicknamed Gengis for the numerous times he had escaped the confines of his cage, leapt over the border into Fricker's garden and launched deadly assaults on the poor creatures that inhabited his wilderness.

Fricker only knew the human occupants of 'Ugly' as Shaz and Shane. Shaz did not talk to coppers, unless it was to issue a curse-filled diatribe on the persecution of the oppressed. However, Shane, as far as Fricker could ascertain, did not, or more likely could not, talk coherently. What they were successful at though was the production of children. At the last count the brood consisted of at least six and possibly seven, ranging in age from approximately five months to eleven. Fricker believed the eldest was called Brad or Brat, the latter seemed more appropriate, but as for the others he had no idea, due to the fact that when called, their names were usually, or so he presumed, heralded or even replaced with one expletive or another. How Shaz and Shane had managed to afford a house in such an exclusive row as his escaped and enraged the socially sensitive Fricker. Feeling his blood pressure rise he made another mental note to ask vice to undertake observations on the dysfunctional duo.

His attention began to wander and after several seconds perusing the gardens on the periphery of his field of vision, Fricker's gaze refocused on Shaz's lawn. Running from the end nearest the house to the furthest accessible point of the garden was a frayed and dirty clothesline. The line, which had obviously seen better days, sagged to almost mud level with the weight of assorted clothes. Nonchalantly Fricker scanned the line until suddenly he averted his eyes in shocked horror.

It couldn't be, he thought, but yes it was, flapping in the light breeze like two deflated weather balloons was the most enormous brassiere Fricker had ever seen.

"Good God, what the hell is that," he exclaimed out loud.

After a second furtive glance his suspicions were confirmed, but clarification of its identity still could not remove the sense of amazement in Fricker's innocent mind. The brassiere hung on the line between a denim mini skirt and a black leather item, from which dangled an array of straps and buckles, so bizarre, the design and use of which baffled him.

Fricker although flabbergasted, found it hard to take his eyes off the offending garments. However, with some effort he extracted himself from the window and stumbled to the kitchen for a restorative cup of tea. Having searched the fridge for some tea bags he eventually returned to his desk, tea in hand, his mind a mass of jumbled thoughts.

God, I must be stressed, he mused, and then closed his eyes in a vain attempt to sleep.

Twenty minutes later his thoughts were still a confused blur, but amongst the myriad of images that appeared randomly was one that reoccurred with increasing regularity. "Denim Bras," he chanted out loud then self-consciously scanned the room in case anyone could have overheard.

Am I turning into the local peeping tom, or was there, he thought, *a deeper significance?* Certainly the Chief Constable thought he was a pervert, he'd said as much, but no Fricker was certain there was something more; although try as he might he could not put his finger on what it was.

CHAPTER 34

Cole and Day were back at Scotswood Manor. Armed with a list of further questions they intended to get to the bottom of why Hillary Smallman was at the canal basin and, more importantly, why she ended up swimming with the fishes.

On their arrival at the Manor, Ball was nowhere to be seen. After a delay of some minutes Clive had opened the door, shown the two constables into Ball's office then disappeared in search of his employer. Left alone and having posted Day outside the door as a lookout, Cole took the opportunity to scan the mound of paperwork that festooned the desk. Ball's well-thumbed copy of *Winnie the Pooh* lay open in the centre, to the right and left were piles of assorted bills and letters.

After flicking through and moving a number of items Cole's attention was drawn to a beige ring binder that had been unearthed by her excavations. She thumbed through it intently.

"Well, well. Just look at this. I knew there was something amiss with the attic. Smallman was always so cagey when I asked her."

Day poked his head back round the corner of the door.

"What have you found, Rita?"

"See the title on this folder, Dorian?"

Day made his way back into the office and having looked at the object in question, nodded in acquiescence.

"Attic Rooms Accounts!" shouted an excited Cole.

Day looked perplexed, but tried hard to grasp the significance of his colleague's discovery.

"Uh huh, and…?" he muttered.

"It tells us everything, keep up, I've been banging on to the DI about the lights in the attic and this folder…" she stopped suddenly in mid-sentence.

"That folder is my private property!" snapped Ball who had appeared almost ghost-like in the now open doorway.

Day took a step backwards; Cole stood her ground. Could this be the same gibbering wreck she and O'Brien had attempted to interview the previous night?

"Yes, it was, but now it's mine, Mr Ball!" rasped an irritated WPC Cole.

Ball's long face puckered as he immediately shed his angry persona and reverted to type.

"I'm sorry," his voice quivering, each word punctuated with loud sobs. "It was just, when I saw you standing there, your fingers all over Hillary's lovely copperplate handwriting I—"

"I get the point, Mr Ball," interjected Cole who cast a swift fierce glance at her almost tearful colleague.

"Put the tissue away, Day, and make some notes!"

Cole resumed her angle of attack. "Right, Mr Ball, let's get to the point. You admit that this is your folder. So tell me why have you never felt it appropriate to inform the authorities of the ten attic rooms and the inmates you incarcerate there?" she paused briefly then continued. "Yet alone tell me, an officer in Her Majesty's Constabulary, when I questioned yourself and Miss Smallman—"

"God rest her soul."

"Don't interrupt, Mr Ball! As I was saying, when I questioned yourself and Miss Smallman on that very same matter."

Ball stifled a howl of despair and attempted to look anywhere other than at the two PCs.

"Let's not prevaricate anymore, Mr Ball, I suggest you make a clean breast of it now! Let's go and see what you have to hide."

Meanwhile, a little over a mile and a half away, on the other side of Hampton le Heath, O'Brien was rekindling old acquaintances with Velda and Stefan. Both had been let out on bail, a decision that, considering the evidence against them, confounded O'Brien. However, he had never been able to understand the vagaries of the Crown Prosecution Service, let alone a bench of muddled magistrates.

Their shop was closed, the blinds were down; but through a slight opening O'Brien could make out the glow of a light somewhere towards the rear of the building. There were a number of things bothering him concerning the initial disappearance of Bronwyn-Jones, in particular the statement by Stefan and Velda that Margaret had "left in a car with a busty blonde" and who was she, or was she a he? Where did they go and why?

O'Brien considered all these questions and his options. After a short delay he put his mind to the latter. *Why change the habits of a lifetime?* he mused, *there was no point in being subtle.* His fist banged loudly and vigorously on the door.

He waited a second or two for a sign of life; with none forthcoming he hammered on the woodwork again. The quiet street reverberated with the noise. A couple of passers-by glanced in O'Brien's direction before scurrying off around the corner whilst a three-legged ginger tom sauntered along the opposite pavement, either oblivious to the commotion or deaf.

O'Brien waited. He strained his ears; he could make out the sound of muffled voices inside the shop. A few moments later he could hear what sounded like shuffling slippers on a solid floor then the rattle of a bolt being drawn.

The door hinges squeaked as it was opened slightly and the now familiar face of Velda peered out into the street.

"Yis, vat can I do for you, Sergeant?" she hissed.

O'Brien's booted foot moved instinctively forward to ensure that the door could not be closed and his gloved hand grasped the edge of the frame and pushed it a little further open.

"Hello, Velda, surprised to see you out and about, I thought you would be in irons."

"I did not know you vere that vay inclined, Sergeant, but just for your information, I only do bondage on a Tuesday night!"

He stifled a smile then leaning forward slightly gave the door a gentle shove.

With a feeling of déjà vu the little Latvian staggered unceremoniously backwards as O'Brien strode into the shop and cast his eye over the barren interior.

The sales floor, previously cluttered with a vast array of astrological paraphernalia, was virtually empty, having been cleared during the forensic investigation by the drug squad. With no obstacles to fall over Velda quickly regained both her footing and some of her composure. Glancing over her shoulder she called out to her partner in crime:

"Stefan darling! Ve have company!"

O'Brien caught the sound of a muffled expletive and the noise of a chair sliding on wooden floorboards coming from the back room.

Five minutes later Stefan, Velda and O'Brien sat around a spindly-legged Formica table in the centre of the shop's dingy kitchen. Stefan was obviously irritated, agitated and nervous. His face twitched regularly and his attention span was almost zero. *Desperate for his next fix*, thought O'Brien. Velda on the other hand was equally irritated by the presence of the police, but more relaxed and controlled.

"Just a couple of questions, that's all."

Stefan grunted, Velda sighed. "Didn't you ask all your stupid questions at the station? Ve told you all ve know then," she snapped.

"I need to know a little more about the day PC Day—"

"I can't remember yesterday, let alone PC Day," drawled Stefan.

"He means, Doris, Stefan darling. You vemember the Crab who turned into a beauty-fal svan in a ved dress."

Stefan grunted again, closed his eyes and with an abstract smile on his face proceeded to fall asleep.

O'Brien sighed; *this*, he thought, *was going to be hard work.*

Giving up on Stefan he focused his attention on Velda and against his better instincts adopted a conciliatory approach.

"You remember, Velda, when you first met young Doris, PC Day as he was then, he asked you if you knew Margaret or Martin as he/she was known and you said he/she had left in a car with a busty blonde."

"Margaret, Martin, Doris, Day! So many names; who are all these peoples?" wailed Velda.

Conciliation was short lived. O'Brien brought his hand down on the table with a resounding bang. Stefan surfaced enough from his coma to emit a "hey man, who let the elephants in?" before descending once more into oblivion whilst Velda placed her head in her hands and began to sob.

"I can't take any more, it's not fair he's alvays out of it," she said pointing at Stefan, "and I, all I do is cook, clean, roll his joints! He is a…" she hesitated; the sobs abated then she continued with venom. "Zirga galva! Es neesmu nekas, bet vergs!"

Whatever it meant, O'Brien hadn't heard language expressed so virulently since his days as a squaddie. He waited for her to continue; she didn't immediately, instead she turned her attention away from Stefan and focused on O'Brien.

"Zirga galva!" she repeated and looked at him with a glare of pure feminist hatred. "You are all the same, you men, users, now get out, I have nothing to tell you, I know nothing, get out!"

Like all ex-army personnel O'Brien knew when to make a tactical withdrawal. He backed away through the shop area pursued by Velda who continued to eject expletives on men, the police and life in general as though they were going out of fashion. O'Brien reached the door and opened it. *One last try*, he thought. "Are you sure there was nothing that you remember about Margaret?" he asked.

"Zirga galva!" she almost spat the words out, her face puce with pent up anger. "I told you it all before, I know nothing! She left with the blonde in a blue car! I told you all this before now get out!"

O'Brien took the hint. In an instant he was standing in the street, the door slammed shut behind him, a grin as broad as the Cheshire Cat's across his face.

So they left in a blue car, did they? he mused. *The plot begins to thicken!*

He consulted his notes. "Next stop Mr Chow's Pagoda Dragon," he said out loud, then realising that talking to himself made him look like a mad man he turned on his heels and made his way back to his car.

Chapter 35

Fricker, recumbent across his tan sofa, had spent the last hour cogitating. So many thoughts were wandering through his brain that he thought his head was full of cotton wool. Why would anyone want to kill him was one of the many questions he asked himself. There was no rhyme or reason to any of the weird happenings that dominated the past week; why had Bronwyn-Jones killed Maitland and Fanshaw and who had killed Bronwyn-Jones and now Smallman?

The phone rang, a trill bleep of immensely irritating pitch.

"What the…!" He paused, picked up the receiver and listened.

"I'm so glad you are alright, when I heard you had been suspended the most bizarre traumatic images and visions came to mind! The thought of my little Gilesy hanging pendulum-like from a banister; the mere idea made my mascara run."

"Who's speaking?" enquired a still confused and befuddled Fricker.

"Giles darling, it's me, Pauline."

"Oh Pauline, yes how are you?" he replied; unsure whether to be pleased or concerned, bearing in mind the ups and downs of their still fledgling relationship.

"I am well, Giles darling, have you seen anything more of your reporter friend?" she asked then continued her sentence without waiting for a reply. "Meet me for a drink, eight this evening would be good; how about the Reckless Hedgehog on the bypass?"

Fricker was stunned, he had not expected another invitation but obediently desperate as always, he said yes and she hung up.

Cole and Day followed Ball out of the office into the hall and up to the first floor landing.

Two minutes later they rounded the final corner of an increasingly constricted stairwell and entered the attic through an old metal-studded wooden door. Ball flicked a light switch. An old fluorescent tube reluctantly oscillated into life revealing a long corridor, its walls covered in cobwebs and damp flaking paint. The corridor was flanked on both sides by similar studded doors. Each door had a small square grill approximately two thirds of the way up. Cole and Day hesitated, then Ball led the way, the noise of their approach elicited a cacophony of shrieks and wailing from behind the closed doors. This was followed by the appearance, through most of the grills, of thin, bony waving arms that clawed at the light as though desperate for food, company or salvation.

"Oh my God!" whispered Cole.

"Aggh help me! It's just like the attic, when I was kidnapped," wailed Day, who immediately turned on his heels and made for the exit.

Ball stood silently still, a solitary tear weaving its way down his long gaunt face. "I'm so sorry. So sooo sorry," he droned.

Ignoring his bleating Cole brushed past him and reaching the first door peered past the flailing arm into the room. Despite being only lit by the light from the corridor and a shaft of light from a high up barred window Cole could make out a small single bed, a basic dressing table and wardrobe. She drew back and her eyes focused on the small figure, which, having removed its arms from the grill had retreated to sit on the edge of the bed. She, as Cole assumed it was a woman, must have been in her late eighties and was painfully emaciated, wearing only a thin polyester nightdress, cotton shawl and a pair of stained fluffy slippers. She stared pleadingly at the young WPC and mouthed the words help me.

Cole turned the handle and rattled the latch; the door was locked.

"Where's the bloody key, Ball?"

Ball sat slumped against the wall on a small wooden stool; other than the rhythmic movement of his shoulders, as they moved up and down in unison with his sobs, he was almost motionless.

The wailing continued unabated and Cole turned towards him her face contorted with rage. She viewed him with undisguised disgust and having received no response to her demand for the key she lost all control.

Grabbing him by the lapels of his tweed jacket she lifted him off his stool and pushed him vigorously against the wall of the corridor. Both were immediately immersed in a shower of paint flakes and cobwebs as Ball stood, wedged like a pit prop between the lowest point of the ceiling and the dust strewn stone floor.

Cole's arm was at full stretch and firmly clamped around his turkey-like neck.

She glared up at Ball along its length.

"Look, you half-baked apology for a man. Get me the bloody keys for these rooms now or I'll use your scrawny frame as a skeleton key!" she rasped.

Ball, now puce and sweating, attempted to mutter something in response, but he was unable to release any words.

The noise in the corridor continued; each inmate added to the din by banging tin plates and cutlery against the bars of the grills and Cole began to sense that Ball was starting to go limp.

A tap on her shoulder brought her back to reality and she turned, releasing, as she did, her grip on Ball's throat. A pale PC Day stood quivering behind her.

"Best let him go, Rita," he said. "We won't find the keys if he's dead and we certainly don't want another body, do we?"

Rita nodded.

"They're in the left-hand drawer of my desk, with a fob marked Attic," croaked Ball who then slumped gasping to the floor.

Having retrieved the key, Cole and Day set about releasing the occupants of the attic. Upon opening the door to one elderly lady's room Cole found her sitting, unmoving on the edge of her bed.

With a bony finger she beckoned the WPC over. Cole bent down. "It's alright, love, we'll have you out of here very soon," she said. The old lady stared with a slightly vacant but menacing look, she grabbed Cole's sleeve and pulled her towards the bed. "I'd bite you if I had my teeth in!" she rasped through empty gums. Startled, Cole leapt backwards and exited the room. By now some inmates had stumbled out into the corridor, others, too frail or too shocked but luckily docile, sat immovable on the edge of their small beds. Cole calmly, but following her recent close encounter, carefully reassured each one whilst Day summoned help. Before long a small crocodile of fragile, confused senior citizens was led and carried down the narrow wooden stairs to freedom.

O'Brien, as the only senior officer available, had, on receiving the call, immediately left his meeting with Mr Chow. The inscrutable Chinaman had not been able to, or certainly did not want to, provide any additional information to the police. He had taken some delight in regaling O'Brien with the story of DI Fricker's visit to the Pagoda Dragon with Pauline Petrie, but when it came to why he was at the canal basin on the afternoon of Hillary Smallman's death he had nothing more to add to his "I was looking for some rainbow trout for the chef's special."

O'Brien was not convinced, but as he drove into the car park at Scotswood Manor his thoughts turned to the new revelations regarding Donald S Ball. He had already passed two ambulances as he drove down the drive and a further six stood immobile, doors ajar and lights flashing outside the Manor. Struggling to find space to park he abandoned his vehicle and bounded up the steps to the already open main door.

"Right, Cole," he barked as she greeted him in the hall. "What on earth has been going on this time?"

Cole quickly enlightened her superior and led him through to the office, where a dejected and despondent Ball sat handcuffed to PC Day.

O'Brien drew up a chair and viewed the man before him. It was obvious he'd had a bad week; his usually pale face had taken on an even greyer complexion, dark circles surrounded his eyes and any spark of life his sombre features may have harboured had been well and truly snuffed out.

"Okay, Ball, let's have the whole story, the truth from the beginning," stated O'Brien.

The room went quiet; PC Day poised, pen in hand, notebook on desk, coughed nervously and then the floodgates opened.

Once started Ball could not stop, he spilled the story right from the start. Their desire for a static caravan in Cleethorpes, the need for more money, then Hillary's wonderful idea; or at least Ball thought it had seemed to be a wonderful idea at the time. He went on; "Why not," Hillary had said, "make use of the attic rooms?" A number of the long-term residents had either been deserted or forgotten by their relatives and having noticed over a period of time that they never had any visitors, they both agreed that nobody would miss them if they disappeared.

"What about the other residents, their friends?" asked Cole.

Ball stifled a laugh. "Friends, these people don't have friends. Our inmates are like goldfish, three minutes and they've forgotten what day it is let alone who they were talking to at breakfast."

Ball continued at pace; "We gradually moved ten of the most neglected residents up to the attic, thereby freeing ten standard flats for immediate occupation and there was no shortage of takers. Money was pouring in and when one of the attic oldies died we made another 'disappear' upstairs. As they were still officially on our books the doctor who attended assumed nothing untoward and anyway they never did a head count!"

By now Ball was almost laughing hysterically; the relief of getting it all off his chest had unleashed a range of emotions from sorrow to elation and having opened Pandora's box O'Brien took the opportunity to pursue Ball even further.

"So why was Hillary at the canal basin?" he asked.

Ball went quiet. A dejected look of sadness swept over his face; however, with the exception of PC Day, who loved a good rom-com, there was no sympathy in the room for either Ball or Smallman.

"She was being harassed, blackmailed!" said Ball quietly.

"Blackmailed? By whom?" enquired Cole.

"I really don't know, there were phone calls, I asked her; I said, sweetkins, who was that? But she wouldn't say, only that there was a woman who had found out about the rooms. It had gone on for about a week or so and it was all getting too much for poor Hil—"

He stopped, sobbed a little more, composed himself then continued.

"She said she'd had enough, she could be quite spiky at times. She said she was going to meet her and sort it all out, get to the bottom of it were her words."

"She certainly did that" interjected Cole absentmindedly, as a vision of Smallman's face emerging from the depths of the canal flicked through her mind.

O'Brien shot her an irritated look, but it was too late. Ball once more dissolved into a cacophony of sobs, wails and tears matched only in their disharmony by the accompanying howls of a now distraught PC Day.

Ignoring the noise O'Brien persisted. However, despite using a rare mixture of tact and manipulation he managed only to glean a small amount of extra information.

Slowly, reluctantly Ball gradually divulged how Smallman had fed the attic residents on leftovers from the kitchen and to avoid discovery had taken on the task of cleaning the rooms. Then the trickle of facts had dried up. After a short interlude on the off chance Ball might begin again, O'Brien exasperatedly called an end to the interview and Day and Ball, both gibbering uncontrollably, left for the cells at Headquarters.

"Nice one, Cole," rasped O'Brien having watched them leave in a waiting police car. "We were getting on fine until you set him off again."

"Sorry, Sarge."

"Never mind," he continued. "We're one step closer. All we need now is to find out who the wretched blackmailer is!"

CHAPTER 36

Nothing had changed since Pauline Petrie's unexpected telephone call. Fricker continued to mooch about his lounge in distracted confusion. Somewhere, he knew it, in the furthest recesses of his puzzled brain lurked the answer to everything; but try as he might he could not set it free.

It didn't help that he was missing Rita Cole; her shapely form regularly floated across his mind's eye as he wondered what she was doing.

It was when he was immersed in a particularly interesting vision involving white sandy beaches and bikinis that the shrill voice of the telephone jolted him from his musings.

Having left endless messages on his answer machine Fricker assumed it must be Dr Schruff. He bounded to the phone; "Doctor, it's you at last. You don't know how much I've needed to talk."

There was a pause at the other end of the line.

"Hello, Doctor S?" said Fricker.

"'Ello," responded a voice that, in its confused tones, held more of a hint of the Mediterranean than gruff Germanic grammar.

"'Ello, Inspector Fricker, is that you?"

"Oh God."

He took a deep intake of breath, paused then toyed with replacing the receiver. The realisation quickly dawned that the voice at the other end of the line was not the illusive Dr Schruff, but instead that of his nemesis Jessica Garcia Aldoraz Dominguez.

Fricker started to feel sick; he hadn't seen her since the church and the last time he spoke to her was prior to the debacle at the canal basin. *She was*, he thought, *the last person he wanted to talk to.*

"It's you, oh God, it's you again," he rasped.

"Ah Inspector Fricker, it is you, you blaspheme, I know it you now. You must 'elp me please."

Fricker's heart sank; he reflected that every contact, every meeting he'd had with the Spaniard had ended badly. As if two attempts to run him over were not enough, there were the photographs. Oh no, the photographs; Fricker's inner sickness turned to anger. This woman had ruined his life and now she wanted 'elp!

His pent up frustration began to boil over. "Look, Dominguez, you short arsed little—" he began, but his tirade was short lived.'

"Do not be angry, Inspector Fricker, I not short arsed, I long bodied, short legged; however, that not matter. You 'elp me, I tell you who killed the cook see."

Fricker gasped. "You know who killed Bronwyn-Jones?" he asked.

"Si, but I can no tell you now. You me meet at the Scotswood Manor say eight o' the clock."

"Jessica," he simpered, changing his tone in an instant. "I cannot—" But the phone was already dead.

Fricker slumped onto his settee and reflected on the conversation. She knew who had killed the cook. When she told him he would be very close to solving the crimes. He would be reinstated and lauded as the great detective he knew he was.

His elation, however, was short-lived and the sick feeling in the pit of his stomach returned. How was he to explain to Pauline that he couldn't make his date?

Fricker's mind went into overdrive; a myriad of excuses poured from every underused corner.

"I'm ill, I'm washing my hair, I've been run over," he bleated as he paced around the lounge analysing the options. *The latter certainly seemed plausible,* he thought, *bearing in mind his recent experiences, but maybe I'm dead would be a better and more realistic excuse.* He mused; *it would definitely be more accurate.* Particularly as when she found out, he imagined he would be!

It took Fricker another ten minutes of mental anguish and a large scotch before his loins were girded sufficiently for him to pick up the telephone and dial.

At Hampton le Heath O'Brien once again set about reviewing the facts; he stood arms folded facing his team. Behind him was a large flip chart, festooned with a multicoloured array of words and interlinked lines, squiggles and crossings out. Having returned from incarcerating Ball, a now emotionally composed PC Day and the ever-enthusiastic WPC Cole sat on the only two available chairs near the door whilst a beaming Sergeant Robson perched on the corner of the desk. O'Brien had seconded a delighted Robson to the case; partially in recognition of his finding PC Day, but mainly as there was no one else available to help.

The search for the illusive blackmailer had still left them stumped. O'Brien was summing up, having waded through the facts relating to the murders of Maitland and Fanshaw by the now deceased and decomposed Bronwyn-Jones.

"Someone had forced or persuaded Bronwyn-Jones to murder the two residents, then got rid of her. Langton had been on the hunt for the alleged missing gold; Ball and Smallman had been mistreating the oldies and had then been blackmailed. Was this the same blackmailer or another one? Someone had twice tried to kill DI Fricker to keep him quiet and the same or another someone had then killed Smallman."

"Didn't the DI overhear someone trying to force the ugly reporter to make her keep him quiet?" queried Cole.

"Yes, that's true, Rita. She was trying to blackmail the DI too I seem to remember. It's a right mess, isn't it, Sarge?" stated a bewildered PC Day.

"I would say it's a confused, discombobulation of disorganised factual and fictitious data," interrupted Cole, whose attempt to continue was then cut short by an alert Sergeant O'Brien.

"Quiet! This is where we are. As we were talking to Mr Ball, Sergeant Robson here was looking into the wills of both Fanshaw and Maitland."

Robson beamed.

"It would appear," continued O'Brien, "that whilst Maitland had very little in the way of assets, Madam Fanshaw was a fairly wealthy woman."

"Who stands to inherit from Fanshaw?" asked Day.

O'Brien was momentarily stunned by what for Day was a very sensible question.

"Well, PC Day, thank you for asking. It would appear that about ninety percent of her wealth has been left to an obscure mission station in Papua New Guinea, a small bequest has gone to her old primary school and the tiny residue went to her niece Pauline Petrie."

"Um, no motive there," continued an enlightened Day.

"It would seem not," confirmed O'Brien, still a little staggered by Day's metamorphosis into a real policeman and keen to understand why.

"Are you alright, Day?"

"Very well, thank you, Sarge, I've realised that if we are going to help the DI we all need to do our best and that is what I hope to do."

"I think they call it an epiphany, Sarge," commented Cole.

"I'd call it a bloody miracle! However, it's very much appreciated and long overdue. Okay team this is what we need to do: Scotswood Manor is pretty safe, there is only Clive left from the original staff; the rest are either in custody or dead. I believe the authorities have installed a temporary manager by the name of Adrienne Weybourne to oversee the few remaining guests. By all accounts she is a formidable woman in more ways than one so we should not need to worry. However, just to be on the safe side I want you, Cole and PC Day, to call in later this evening to check all is in order. In the meantime I think we need to have a word with the reporter from the *Argos*. What's her name?"

"Garcia Aldoraz Dominguez, I believe, Sarge," responded Day.

"Yes, exactly, well done, Day. You and Cole go and see if you can locate her, bring her in for questioning. She must have some idea who the blackmailer is."

"What about me, Sergeant O'Brien?" enquired a slightly deflated Robson.

"Oh, you Sergeant Robson. You man the phones here just in case; I have to go and talk to the Chief Constable about the case and DI Fricker."

CHAPTER 37

Fricker's ears were still ringing despite the substantial passage of time since he had spoken to Pauline Petrie. As he nursed his beloved Colin along the now dark leafy lanes towards Scotswood Manor he repeated the conversation out loud in a vain attempt at self-help. It had started well, she had sounded almost civil to him when he had first made contact. But as before, when he mentioned the reporter's name and the fact their meeting clashed it was like he had unleashed the four horses of the apocalypse. "Pauline dear, you don't understand, it's not that I don't want to see you, it's just that Miss Dominguez needs to talk," and that was the catalyst he mused. "Miss dumpy wants to talk," she said. "I'll give you TALK! You spineless apology for a man! Talk, I'll give you something to talk about," she raged on, then issued an expletive-laden tirade and slammed the phone down with venom.

Fricker was still in shock when he pulled up on the all too familiar gravel car park. Checking his watch he realised he was five minutes late, but despite that he decided to sit in the comforting confines of Colin's leather-clad interior and gather his thoughts.

Scotswood Manor looked eerily dark; its shadowy grey walls, which he had seen at all hours of the day over the past week, seemed to fill him with a deep sense of foreboding. Perhaps Pauline had been right, perhaps he was a spineless apology for a man. Fricker cajoled himself to get a grip and tentatively climbed out of the car. He shivered in the now chilly evening air, and gave Colin a reassuring stroke along its polished wing. Walking slowly towards

205

the main door he glanced around the dimly lit car park; parked in the corner nearest the house was a small white hatchback. It had the words Hampton le Heath Home Care Agency and a cartoon of a rather rotund, apron-clad care worker festooned across its boot. To its right was a small blue car, which, Fricker noted, appeared to have been abandoned in some haste rather than parked. A little way away, highlighted by one of the few car park lamps, stood a bright yellow Vespa-type motorcycle.

He quickened his pace, reached the door and went to press the doorbell.

Fricker realised immediately there was no need. The wooden door to Scotswood Manor was unlocked and ajar.

O'Brien's mood, as he sat in the hallway outside Chief Constable Hogarth's office, was not good. It was nearly eight o'clock and he was feeling the effects of a long exhausting day. An earlier telephone call from Cole and the now strangely efficient Day revealed that they had failed to locate the Spanish reporter. It appeared that her exasperated editor at the *Evening Argos* had not seen her for two days and was on the verge of mailing her P45. He had, however, furnished them with her last known address, a run down bed and breakfast on the north side of Hampton le Heath, but a visit there had also drawn a blank. The landlady could only tell them that she had last seen her earlier in the day, driving off unsteadily with two bags across her shoulders on a bright yellow scooter. O'Brien finished their conversation by reminding them that they needed to call in at Scotswood Manor later that evening. He was just musing on a further fruitless exchange he had then had with Sergeant Robson when the intercom above him crackled into life and summoned him into Hogarth's office.

Godfrey Hogarth was showing signs of the strain of life since O'Brien last saw him. His hair, or at least what was left of it, had an almost universal tinge of grey and he looked tired, immensely tired.

"Right, O'Brien," he said in a resigned voice. "Let's get to the point. Have you solved any of these murders?"

O'Brien took a large intake of breath and started at the beginning.

Fricker pushed the door open and peered into the dark unlit hallway. *Strange, very strange*, he thought, then glanced at the luminous dial of his watch to reassure himself that it was only ten past eight and not midnight.

"Hello, Mr Ball, are you there?" he tentatively enquired, then walked slowly across the tiled floor to the door to Ball's office. It was shut. Fricker knocked twice, the sound echoed around the hall and from somewhere higher up in the house he heard the unmistakable sound of a slamming door and what he thought were running feet. This he chose to ignore, choosing instead to seek out the vicar before investigating further.

With no light showing under the door and having obtained no response from within the office he opened the door and entered. Almost at once he stumbled and half-fell across a large inanimate object. The thing appeared to take up all of the floor space between the door and the desk. It felt soft and lumpy, and Fricker's hands recoiled in horror when further blind fumbling discovered what appeared to be the flabby contours of a person's face.

He let out a shriek of horror then stood bolt upright, reversed towards the door and through a stroke of good fortune managed to lay hands on the light switch.

"Aggh! Oh my God," he squealed as the flickering strip light revealed the previously unidentified object. An enormous tabard-clad woman lay flat on her back in front of the desk with what appeared to be an ornate paper knife imbedded in her chest.

Fricker felt sick, averting his eyes from the gruesome sight before him, he leant against the doorframe to re-gather his thoughts.

Half a minute later he felt well enough to look again. She was, he surmised, a large woman who had been in her time extremely ugly and now without a shadow of a doubt she was dead.

To be doubly sure Fricker bent down and checked the pulse in her neck. While doing so he noticed the corner of a badge protruding from under one of the many folds in her clothing. He read it out loud, "Adrienne Weybourne Care Manager." Almost instantaneously an ear-piercing scream shattered the unearthly quiet of the house.

Fricker almost jumped out of his skin, Adrienne Weybourne didn't move.

"What the hell was that?" he asked himself then turned quickly, left the office and waited motionless in the hallway.

He didn't have long to wait. A second scream punctuated the silence followed by the words, " 'Elp me someone, 'elp me pleese!"

In an instant Fricker recognised the appalling pronunciation of Jessica Garcia Aldoraz Dominguez. The voice appeared to come from the same vicinity as the previous noises and assuming that to be higher up in the house Fricker raced up the stairs one at a time. Rounding the corner onto the first floor landing he ran straight into two old ladies dressed in matching white dressing gowns. One carried a small brass candleholder from which the light of a tall white candle lit their pale faces.

"Health and safety, girls," wheezed a surprised and out of breath Fricker. "Naked flames can cause fires! What are you doing wandering about in the dark?"

"The lights on the landing seem to have fused, Inspector," said the slightly taller of the two who then continued. "My name is Edna and this is my friend Hilda, we heard a noise and as neither of us could agree as to what note it was we came out to see if we could hear better in the corridor. The acoustics are much better here I find, don't you, Hilda?"

Hilda had just opened her mouth to formulate a reply when a further scream echoed down an adjacent stairwell.

"There, Hilda, a B flat and I do believe she's a contralto," stated Edna.

"Where does that lead?" asked Fricker pointing at the entrance. No answer was forthcoming. Fricker momentarily gazed in disbelief at the two women then surmised that they were obviously away with the fairies. Taking the candle from Edna's grasp he bellowed at them not to move, then, ignoring their protestations, climbed up the narrow stairs.

Very shortly he found himself in the same dark corridor where, unknown to him, Cole and Day had previously discovered the incarcerated residents. As Fricker moved hesitantly along the passageway the spluttering light of the candle revealed that all the wooden studded doors on each side were open. All around there was the pervasive smell of damp and decay and, with every movement, cobwebs brushed his face and hands. His foot caught a large black object on the floor, which further investigation by candlelight revealed to be a camera. Fricker began to sweat. "Strange," he said in an attempt at self-reassurance. "No sign of life."

Many mishaps over the years had proved that it was a Fricker family failing to speak too soon. As soon as he uttered the last syllable a previously unseen door at the end of the corridor was flung open to reveal an all too familiar figure in the entrance.

"Pauline!" he squawked at the sight of the black lycra-clad figure.

"Thought I'd join you for your little meeting with Senorita Dumpy. You don't mind do you, Giles?"

Fricker felt more than a little uncomfortable as he edged towards the open door. From it a sharp cold draught swept down the corridor making his paltry candle flicker vigorously.

"Pauline, where is Miss Dominguez?"

Pauline Petrie took a step backwards and beckoned Fricker to join her on what he could now make out was a relatively small area of flat roof at the edge of the main structure. The roof was surrounded by what appeared to be a low stone balcony.

"Oh, how sweet, are you missing her already? You pathetic creature!"

"Pauline, there was nothing between us, it was only

professional; she was going to tell me who killed Bronwyn-Jones," Fricker replied nervously as he emerged into the cool night air.

"God, you're thick. I know all that. Why do you think I'm here?"

Fricker did not answer. He glanced around. In a corner nearest to the slope of the main roof, hunched up in a ball, sat the sobbing reporter. She gently rocked backwards and forwards cradling in her arms a small holdall and the large black bag containing her precious twin spool tape recorder.

"Did you not see the body downstairs?" he asked either one of them, but in his own mind he already knew the answer.

Pauline Petrie answered first. "So you found the fat old bat? I'd better come clean then, Inspector. After all, you and the snivelling Spaniard will soon be joining her in never never land!"

Fricker shivered and looked towards the doorway. Pauline Petrie, however, was ahead of him and had, having extracted the candle from his shaking fingers, positioned herself in front of the exit.

"Don't even bother to think, Giles, it's not your style. I blackmailed Bronwyn-Jones or shall we call it Martin, as that's what he preferred, to kill Aunty Connie. I had plenty on the cross-dressing cook as you can imagine. Trouble was he/she was number blind and battered the wrong old biddy. Not that that mattered too much, made it look like there was a serial killer on the loose. After that she had to go. So I invited her to the Fantasy Club, she liked it there, then bathed her in acid and buried her in the compost heap. Had it not been for the wretched dog everyone would have thought she had done it and run away, disappeared.

"Then why involve me?" queried Fricker.

"Well, at that point I thought you might be an intelligent copper. You might know the saying "keep your friends close but your enemies closer." Anyway I discovered I was wrong, but by then I had already put the screws on your little fat friend. Turns out she was a bit of an illegal alien, overstayed her original visa or some such misdemeanour. So anyway I got her to embarrass you, get you off the case, I even paid her money, felt a bit sorry for her. You see I have got a heart, Giles," she laughed.

"So it was you at the church?"

"Full marks, Detective Inspector Fricker. Had I known how dense you were I needn't have bothered. Then it all went pear-shaped. I discovered Aunty Connie, the miserable cow, had left me nothing, well just a couple of thousand. That wouldn't have paid the interest on my credit card bill let alone a deposit on my next visit to my surgeon."

She thrust her extravagant chest towards Fricker who recoiled precariously close to the low railing.

"These babies cost seventeen grand, Giles, so you can see my need. Anyway I digress, I needed another cash cow and luckily for me who should I discover had been cooking the books and hiding old dears in the roof but little Miss butter wouldn't melt in her mouth Smallman and her inane fiancé, Donald."

"What did they do?" asked Fricker who had decided that his only hope of escape was to keep her talking.

"Fraud, neglect, you name it. Anyway it's cold and I need to be getting along, so to finish off, Giles, so to speak, I blackmailed them. Sadly though it ended before I could achieve very much. Smallman turned out to be a feisty little hag, she did not want to play ball. I arranged to meet her at the canal basin just before you and your fat friend, thought I could get you incriminated for her murder. It worked like clockwork. She sank like a stone, but I couldn't resist trying to run you over again, just so funny to see you dive for cover."

"What was Mr Chow doing there?" queried Fricker.

"Oh Chow, no idea, looking for rainbow trout I ass—"

She stopped in mid-flow her eyes darting towards the main drive, three storeys below. "Oh shit!" she exclaimed.

Fricker sighed in relief as the headlights of what appeared to be a police vehicle moved slowly into the car park.

"Best get a move on then," she snapped. Then added, "Oh by the way, stabbing the blob downstairs was the easiest. Like

211

puncturing a balloon," she laughed again, but this time the laugh had more of a maniacal edge to it.

Placing the candle on the floor just inside the open door, she moved purposely towards her victims.

Cole and Day hopped out of their car and surveyed the dark building in front of them. There was no sign of life.

"All tucked up in bed," suggested Cole.

"Looks like it, let's be off then," retorted Day who as ever was keen to get back into the warmth of his car. They both turned and were just about to open the doors when an ear-splitting shout rent the air.

"HELP! Help, up here!"

Cole and Day swivelled on their heels just in time to catch sight, high up on the roof of the building, of the unmistakable profile of DI Fricker, silhouetted against the light of the moon.

"Call Sergeant O'Brien now!" barked Day. "I'm going in."

Cole stood for a moment, both flabbergasted and impressed as the new style PC was already disappearing up the steps of the main door, two at a time.

Dominguez was now standing up and had joined Fricker, who, aided by the moonlight, had backed away to the furthest point of the flat roof.

"Look, Pauline," he simpered in an attempt to buy a little more time. "Can't we just talk about this? After all I'm sure there are extenuating circumstances; messed up childhood, inferiority complex—"

"Esta loca!" interjected Dominguez.

"Yes, very good. Insanity. You will probably qualify for that one."

Pauline Petrie stopped in her tracks disturbed by a strange shuffling sound from inside the attic.

"Shut it, and stay there!" she barked. Turning on her heels she moved quickly to the open door.

"Who the hell are you?" she snapped to someone that neither Fricker nor Dominguez could see.

"Oh, sorry to disturb you," came the hesitant reply. "I'm Edna and this is my companion Hilda. We've been looking for our candle, the lights have gone out and the very rude policeman stole it. But look we've found it now."

With a glare that would have melted the polar icecaps Petrie snapped, "Put the bloody candle down and beat it, you pair of old harpies!"

This was all too much for Hilda. She swooned sideways, lost her balance and knocked the lit candle from her partner's grasp before collapsing on the dusty floor.

In an instant the years of discarded rubbish, crumbling laths and old bird nests that filled the recesses of the roof void were alight. Edna screamed, Hilda grunted and Pauline Petrie stepped back out onto the roof, slammed the door and locked it.

Petrie turned towards Fricker and the now cowering Dominguez, her face contorted in fury. She held the key aloft, taunting the quivering pair; then dropped it into her lycra-clad cleavage.

We will never find that in silicone valley, mused Fricker, surprised that he could still find something to be funny in this dire situation. However, his humour did not last for long; flames were now flickering through the grey slate roof and acrid smoke was beginning to envelop their small sanctuary.

Fricker looked around nervously; above the cracking of splintering wood, he thought he could hear the sound of sirens. Perhaps, if he could spin this out for another five minutes he might get out alive.

Down below in the car park Sergeant O'Brien, the Chief Constable and an elderly bearded gentleman of foreign extraction joined WPC Cole. "This is Dr Schruff," stated O'Brien as he introduced the newcomer.

Dr Schruff rubbed his bleary eyes and nodded. Having only

returned that evening from his sabbatical in Bratislava he was weary and a little unhappy at being summoned to the scene.

"I collected this for you," said O'Brien as he delved in his jacket pocket and extracted a plastic bag, its contents a mixture of slime, fur and some unidentifiable material.

"Ugh, vot ist this?" enquired the doctor.

"I got it out of the DI's desk," replied O'Brien. "When Cole explained the situation I thought he might need it."

"Ya, good thinking, I see, yes now; it is Giles's severed rabbit's foot and putrefied Bockwurst sausage. It gives him comfort."

Dr Schruff affectionately patted the packet and placed it in his black leather shoulder bag.

The car park was now congested with a wide array of emergency services vehicles, their occupants looking up, incredulous but powerless as the once imposing building was engulfed with flames and smoke.

High on the roof three silhouetted figures stood out against the backdrop of destruction. "He'll swing for this!" ranted the Chief Constable as his mood fluctuated between anger and despair. "I'll have him certified at the very least. Cole, get social services on the phone. Tell them to bring a straightjacket! If he doesn't need one, I will."

"Good idea," interjected Dr Schruff before everyone's attention was diverted towards the main door of the house. Through the billowing smoke, the coughing, spluttering figure of Dorian Day appeared, his thin arms buckling under the minimal weight of the inert but alive body of Hilda.

Edna, Clive and a small crocodile of elderly residents followed him with Martha Nixdorf bringing up the rear, her once silver Zimmer now black and smouldering. The watching crowd burst into spontaneous applause before a posse of paramedics raced to the aid of the singed PC.

Back on the roof the smoke and heat were becoming unbearable;

however, Petrie, exasperated and irritated as a result of the constant interruptions to her plan, was still quite sure she could plant the blame solely at the feet of DI Fricker and with no witnesses, get away scot-free.

Fuelled by this new sense of purpose she strode forward. With one vigorous push Fricker was bundled out of the way. He landed, partially winded, in a heap, straddling a wide valley gutter.

"Thought I would do the short one first," she said. "You can watch her bounce."

Fricker, stunned and in pain, looked on in despair as with Amazonian strength Petrie picked up Dominguez and dangled her over the balcony.

"Ples, this bags they are so heavy, please a do not drop me," bleated the reporter as she hung over the void. Her arms, legs and bags swinging through the smoke.

Petrie laughed once then released her grip.

In an instant Jessica Garcia Aldoraz Dominguez disappeared from view and Petrie turned towards the quivering figure of Fricker.

She made one step forward then stopped abruptly.

"Ples, this bags they are so heavy, please 'elp me," came the unmistakable voice from over the parapet.

"Bloody hell, won't anything go right today?" rasped Petrie as she turned and peered over the edge. "Oh Christ, her bag's caught on an overflow pipe," she whined, then with more than a hint of scorn added, "Don't worry, Jessica, I'll soon have you off."

With the flames and noise all around becoming more intense Petrie leant over the railing, poking and prodding in an attempt to free the wedged bags.

Noting that she was significantly distracted Fricker took his chance.

Masked by the smoke he moved forward and hesitantly pushed her in the small of her back. It had no effect other than to make her lean on the edge of the railing.

She half-turned towards him smirking.

"Not hard enough, Giles, I told you that you were a spineless apology for a man."

Her glee was short-lived, though; the contemptuous smile turned to one of pure panic as the top rail of the stone balcony wobbled then tipped and, aided by her top-heavy proportions, Pauline Petrie plummeted to the ground below.

An ear-splitting scream reverberated off the walls of Scotswood Manor and the vehicles in the car park below. Heads turned, but nothing was visible through the smoke and flames.

In an ambulance a frail old lady sat beside a stretcher, holding the hand of her companion of over thirty years.

"Did you hear that?" she asked.

"Yes, that was a top C," croaked Hilda, "definitely a top C."

"Absolutely, dear," replied Edna, who, as her friend closed her eyes for the last time, wiped away the tears that trickled down her cheek.

POSTSCRIPT

Detective Inspector Giles Fricker survived the fire, managing to hold onto the suspended Jessica Garcia Aldoraz Dominguez until the firemen could reach them. Flanked by Dr Schruff and a paramedic he was led away, still smoking, past the gutted remains of Scotswood Manor, to a waiting white van.

Miss Dominguez recovered quickly; having filed her story she was welcomed back to her work as an ace reporter with the *Evening Argos*. All knowledge of her alien status and her role in any criminal events lost with the death of Pauline Petrie.

Fricker's recovery took a little longer. Diagnosed with a myriad of complaints ranging from third-degree burns, smoke inhalation, OCD and a melancholy disposition, he spent the next six months on sick leave, before being absolved by an independent enquiry of any blame in the death of Pauline Petrie and the destruction of Scotswood Manor.

He was subsequently reinstated as head of CID at Hampton le Heath and reunited with his team.

Chief Constable Godfrey Hogarth was as good as his word. Unable to cope with the thought of Fricker's return he took early retirement and admitted himself to a sanatorium in New Mexico.

For his role in the rescue of residents at Scotswood Manor, PC Dorian Day was awarded the Queen's Police Medal for exceptional bravery.